# JUST

# ANOTHER

# MODEL

vesnxx

# DEDICATION

To everyone that kept pushing me to reach my best potential and never gave up on my stubborn personality

# CONTENTS

## Chapter 1 (Becky's POV)

"ARE YOU SHITTING ME RIGHT NOW?"

I was looking at Gareth with wide eyes full of shock.

He was about to fire my ass and ruin my reputation in the world of fashion.

And why?

Because he was a cheating lying asshole!

Let's take a break so I can tell you a bit more about the details, shall we?

Let me first introduce myself.

My name is Rebecka Collins, but everyone calls me Becky and not many even know my full name honestly, that's how rare I use it.

I am or I should say I WAS a model of worldwide proportions.

I love this work.

It gives me the opportunity to see the world, do what I love and get paid for it so I can live a life many would envy me.

But I am not a spoiled brat in any way.

The only downfall to my work is that I rarely see my best friend or my brother, but I guess you can't have it all in my line of work.

Now the ugly part comes.

A few months ago, one of my superiors started showing interest in me.

And honestly, I only had one boyfriend in all the years.

So of course, it was flattering for me.

After a few weeks we started going out.

A dinner here and there, drinks after work hours etc., you get the drill.

A week ago, I finally let him get into my pants.

But mark my words: he said he was single!

So, we were fooling around for a week and suddenly pictures leaked about us being seen around Paris where we were situated at the moment.

I didn't think it was a big deal honestly but like I mentioned, I thought he was single.

And I had no clue the truth was different until today when he confronted me.

His words left a sour taste in my mouth.

He said this thing between us could not continue, which was really ok with me. It wasn't like I was in love or anything.

But what came out of his mouth next led to the response from earlier.

To make the picture clearer I will cite his words.

"You should also quit your job, or I will make sure you lose it. I can't have my wife breathing down my neck because she thinks I am cheating on her."

Now tell me. Does he sound like an asshole or is it just my opinion?

So here we are now.

Destined to either give up my job or wait for Gareth to ruin my life.

I was still staring at him, and I could see all his blood drained from his face at my words.

He was probably hoping I wouldn't hear the part about his wife, but I did hear it.

I've heard it really good.

When there was no response from him even after a minute I had enough.

"You know what? I will write my resignation today, not because of you or because I did something wrong, but because I know you are an asshole who will go to any lengths to make himself look good! And you said you were single, and now I have to pay for your greedy selfish ass!"

He was momentarily taken aback by my words, but I would not wait for his response.

A sharp slap met his left cheek and after a few seconds thought his right one received one as well.

"I hope your wife realizes what kind of a douchebag you are and leaves you for someone better! Because no woman deserves to be cheated and later lied to!"

With those words I stamped away from him and out of the museum where my shooting should take place.

But guess it won't.

I quickly pulled out my phone and dialed the only person I wanted to talk to right now.

She picked up on the second ring.

"Hey Becks. What's up?"

Her voice alone made me feel better and worse at the same time.

Better because I knew she would always be here for me, but worse because I really missed my friend and wanted her to be next to me right now so I wouldn't have to tell her everything while we spoke on the phone.

"Hey Rachel. Guess who is coming home in a few hours?"

A shriek pierced my ears and even though my situation was as fucked as it could be I laughed qt her excitement.

"Are you serious? How did you manage to get some vacation at this time of year? It has always been the busiest season for you! Wait. Becky, what happened? You are not coming back for vacation, are you?"

I chuckled at my bestie. She knew me and my line of work so well.

And she was right. It was the summer season, and those seasons were the busiest in my line of work.

But I guess this summer I can relax.

"No Rach. There's no vacation. I got fired. But I'd like to tell you the details once I land in London. I just wanted to let you know I am coming. And if you could tell Mason as well, I would really appreciate it."

A familiar laugh was heard on the other side of the line, and it made me smile right away.

"Thanks, sis, for thinking about me as well. Just let us know when to pick you up from the airport and we'll be there."

"Thanks guys. You are the best. See you in a few hours."

With those words we disconnected the call.

I still couldn't believe the two most important people in my life were in a happy relationship.

Even though in a way it felt like my world was crashing down, on the other side it felt like I could finally breathe with full lungs.

I decided right there and then, this summer will be one I will remember forever.

Where I will put myself in the first place.

Do all the things I've put off for years, and finally enjoy my time off with my best friend and my brother.

Let's make this summer count.

Chapter 2 (Aron's POV)

Why does it have to rain in London almost every day?

Yeah, yeah.

I know I can move to another city, but I don't want to.

The only person that's close to me lives here.

And that would be my aunt.

You read that correctly.

My mother left me when I was just a baby.

One day she just dropped me on her sister's front porch and never came back.

Not even to check up on me.

I discovered all these things later in my life when I was 15 years old.

My aunt told me to sit down one day when I came from school and told me everything.

She told me how my own mother left me, but pointed out that I am not missing anything. Because she was a manipulative person obsessed with material things. That year we also went to change my last name to McNamara. Aunt said that if I ever succeed in life, which she was sure I would, my mother will track me down and beg for money or even try some nasty games.

So, her leaving me didn't really affect me.

I can't say I was sad, since I don't ever remember the woman that gave birth to me, but it still felt a bit weird. But still I continued to call my aunt mom because that's what she is to me.

She has raised me up into a man that I am today. She was there when I needed a shoulder to cry on, she supported me through every obstacle in life and if it wasn't for her, today I wouldn't be where I am.

Meaning sitting in my office in my own very successful company.

But my life these days felt like there was something missing.

All the time I felt…. lonely.

I was thinking about a solution, and I think it would be great if I got myself a dog.

I live in a house that is not too big, but neither is it small.

It also has a yard and a lot of room to run around.

And most days I have too much free time on my hands, especially since I employed Rachel.

She was a great plus in our company.

She goes through almost all my papers because she knows how much I hate doing it, she picks up the phones…I won't go on anymore because you get my point. She was a gem.

And lucky Mason grabbed her with both his hands and took her for herself.

Not that I ever saw Rachel as anything else as an employee.

But I had eyes and ears, and I knew when a woman was the perfect package.

Just not for me.

You might think since I am so lonely, I might need a girlfriend or maybe at the age of 30 I might be thinking about a wife already.

But my opinion?

Thanks, but no thanks.

Didn't you listen to my story?

My own mother left me with someone else.

So, the only woman in my life that deserved my respect and trust was my aunt.

End of story.

So here I am.

Sitting in my office and just thinking about getting a dog.

Suddenly there's a knock at my door, and at this hour it can only be Rachel.

After I tell her to come in, she opens the door with her signature smile stretched across her face.

"Hey boss. I was just wondering, is there any chance I could go home a bit earlier today? You see Becky is coming home and after 6months of no personal contact I think we are overdue for some catching up."

I was listening to her rambling, seeing how nervous she was because she had to ask for a favor, "Rachel? How many times have you saved my ass since you came to work as my assistant?"

Her face was pure shock and confusion.

"Uhm. I have no idea about saving your ass, but if you mean that when I am here, I work and not twiddle my thumbs then I'd say every day?"

I chuckled at her words. She had a point. She was one of my workers that worked the hardest. Well besides her boyfriend Mason, who was my best programmer on the team. Sometimes I wonder how far we would even manage to climb without him.

"No. I was thinking more about those papers you do daily because you know I hate dealing with them. Then there are those nasty emails that I know you hate but you deal with them anyway. So yes Rachel of course you can take off for the rest of the day."

She gave me the brightest smile I have ever seen, and I couldn't even process everything before she flung her arms around my neck and gave me a literal bear hug.

Just then someone stepped inside my office and there stood Mason.

I could see the jealousy in his eyes even though I've told him a million times that Rachel was nothing more than a friend to me.

He cleared his throat and Rachel straightened her back and ran into Mason's embrace.

"Hey handsome. I've told you Aron is the best boss ever. He gave me the rest of the day off so we can meet with Becky. Shall we?"

As soon as she was by his side, Mason's posture relaxed, and his eyes didn't scream murder anymore.

They both said their goodbyes and Rachel told me to call her in case of an emergency.

Yeah. Not going to happen.

That woman deserves some free time.

So now it was just me and my thoughts.

Right!

I need a dog!

## Chapter 3 (Becky's POV)

Home sweet home.

I never knew coming home after a disastrous few weeks can feel so freaking good.

And you know what's even better?

Seeing two of your favorite people waiting for you with big grins on their faces, and weird as it is, for the first time, they are not arguing.

Must be love.

I practically ran to hug Mason and Rachel.

I knew there was a lot to talk about, but right now the only thing I needed was their love and support.

And they delivered big time.

Rachel almost strangled me, that's how tight her hug was, and Mason, the kind of brother that he was, didn't pass up a chance to ruin my hair just like old times.

Like I said. It's good to be home.

We picked up my luggage well, technically Mason picked it up while me and Rachel gushed over each other about how good we look, how happy Rachel seems, how tanned I am, bla bla bla.

You get the point.

But once we all got piled up in Mason's car the interrogation began. But weirdly, Mason started it.

"Now Becks. Spill the beans. Who needs to be sued, whom do I need to beat up, and do I need to kill someone? Because in that case you two are helping me hide the body."

Rachel and I both stared at him with wide eyes and open mouths.

But the second our eyes met we burst into laughter.

I love my brother. I swear he was the best.

And don't make a mistake.

He definitely would kill a person for me if he thought it was necessary.

And me and Rachel would actually help him.

Because that's just how things were in our family.

We stuck together in good and bad.

Well, let's not get dramatic.

We wouldn't kill anyone in the near future.

Probably.

A smirk was playing on Mason's lips, and I was grateful he managed to break the ice.

I took a deep breath and started talking.

"You see in Paris; I got a new supervisor because Mandy was assigned to another model for this season, so she flew to Mexico the other day. This new supervisor of mine was a man. A scumbag technically speaking. He lied to me. He told me he was single, and he only had eyes for me. Of course, I wasn't going to be easy prey, so I played hard to get. So, a few days ago it felt like he worked enough. And I let him get into my pants."

At my last words Mason made a weird face.

Yeah, yeah, I know it's probably not easy to listen about your sisters' sex life.

But hey, he asked, and I was just giving him an honest answer.

Without any additional explanations I can say in my defense.

I was giving him just the facts.

A smirk still pushed its way to my lips.

It was fun toying with him.

I am still a younger sister so it's my obligation to torture him.

"So, after that he approached me the next day, and told me to either quit my current job or he would destroy my reputation and I would become a homewrecker because asshole dearest had a very jealous wife who was breathing down his neck. And as I later found out, he wouldn't have to do much to destroy me, since his wife was the one who owned the place where the shooting was taking place."

Mason stepped on the brakes and they both turned around to look at me with shock written on their faces.

Suddenly Mason's face became as red as a tomato, and he started to make a U turn.

"Nope. We are going back, and I will be going to Paris. He is a dead man."

A laugh burst out of me.

"Don't Mason. He is not worth it. And besides I needed a break. And he kind of gave me the perfect opportunity. So, let's just get something to eat, shall we?"

After a few minutes of convincing, he finally agreed to let it go. For the moment.

I would take what I could.

We arrived at our favorite dinner in town and went to a booth in the back of the room.

We ordered our food, and I was chatting with Mason, while Rachel looked at something work related.

Suddenly her face paled while she was looking at her phone.

I got a bad feeling in the pit of my stomach.

"Becky you won't like this."

I looked at the screen that she turned my way and there in bold letters was written: Famous model "Becky" taking on a new role-homewrecker?

And that ladies and gentlemen is how you ruin someone's chances to work in their field. Forever.

But strangely...all I could feel was relief.

What was going on with me?

I love my job, I really do.

But now it was time to ask myself the hard questions.

Do I want to have a family one day?

Do I want my life to be full of scandals and traveling, or family and love?

Looking across the table at my best friend and my brother I got my answer.

My career might end in a shitty way, but I still had people that cared about me.

So, I decided.

I looked at them with a huge grin and they returned it with faces full of shock.

They probably thought I went crazy.

Who can blame them? My job was my life until yesterday.

"Don't worry guys. I know it's not a nice way to retire from my line of work. But I think it's the perfect timing. It's time for me to start concentrating on my family and maybe even my love life."

Rachel jumped from her stool and came around the table to give me a hug.

"We will always be by your side babes. And I am so proud of you. Also, we wanted to tell you this in person. We are getting married, and you are my maid of honor."

I looked at her surprised, but once I got over the shock the true screaming began.

We were jumping and laughing and crying, all at once.

And Mason was trying to not become deaf from our screaming.

But who cares.

I would finally get the best sister-in-law a person could ask for.

I guess my life didn't nosedive with my resignation. It just started to go upwards.

## Chapter 4 (Aron's POV)

You see, most days being me is not too bad.

But some days it's pure hell.

Well today was one of those days.

Rachel had her day off, because she was preparing for her wedding, and I was stuck with a phone that was ringing every 5 seconds.

And I am not even exaggerating.

At this pace I wouldn't manage to get a simple check up with my programmers.

And that was something that I could not afford.

So, I quickly pulled out my phone and called Rachel.

Yes, I did feel like a douchebag for doing it while she had her day off, but I needed her help like yesterday.

She picked up the call after only 2 rings.

"Hey boss man. Is it an emergency? I can be there in 15."

A soft smile pushed its way on my lips.

It was the first one today.

Rachel really was one of a kind and I doubt I'd ever find a better assistant.

"No, no, don't stress. But I do have a question for you."

I paused to hear her reaction first, but she surprised me again with no hesitation.

"Shoot."

I chuckled lightly at her.

"Do you by any chance know anyone who would be willing to fill in for you on your days off?"

"Hmmm. Give me a second."

I could hear she cowered the microphone with her hand while she was speaking to someone. But I couldn't hear any words, just murmuring.

After a minute or two she picked it back up.

"Are you still there Aron?"

"Yeah. I am here. Please tell me if you have good news for me. Also, before I forget. Once you get back to work, remind me to give you a raise. I had no idea how fucked up your position in our company was."

She chuckled lightly.

"Don't stress it, Aron. I knew what I signed for and I am not complaining. But to get to the matter at hand. I do have some good news. You remember Mason's sister Becky?"

I dug through my memory for a second before it all clicked.

"The model that came back last week. Yes, I remember you and Mason talking about her. What about her?"

"Well, she retired from her modelling career and is looking for a job. She is willing to cover for me on my days off for the time being and even if no position opens up for her you could at least write her a letter of recommendation, so she gets a bit of a push while she finds her way around London again. What do you say?"

I couldn't believe what I heard.

It sounded perfect, so I grabbed the chance before any of the girls got a chance to change their minds.

"Amazing! Could she start today? That's if you don't need her help of course."

Laughing, she answered my question and made my day ten times more bearable.

"No worries. She will be there in 15. Have a good day boss man."

With those words she hung up and I could finally relax a little.

Only 15 more minutes of hell before help arrives.

I was checking the clock every 10 seconds, counting down the minutes before Becky arrived.

Only a good 10 minutes had passed when there was a knock on my door.

I told the person to come in and at first sight became speechless.

In front of me stood the most beautiful woman I have ever seen.

She was tall, I'd say at least 1,7m if not a few centimeters taller. Long toned legs, and high heels that made them look even longer.

I didn't see her from behind but what I saw from the front looked amazing.

Breasts that were just the right size for a hand full judging from the view I had. She had a soft blue skirt and matching blouse tucked in at the waist.

But once I reached her face the real shock hit me.

The bluest eyes I have ever seen were looking back at me. A cute nose that was a bit upturned and mouth that looked more than kissable.

And those blond hair.

They reached all the way down to her ass and my mind couldn't stop the thought of her on all fours while I wrapped that hair around my hand and pound into her.

But her words broke my lust induced state in seconds.

"Hey. My name is Becky. Rachel sent me as her back up."

How in hell was she related to Mason?

I guess shock must be evident on my face because she suddenly chuckled.

"I know I look nothing like Mason. I took my appearance from dad's side while he got our mother's. But I swear we are brother and sister."

I shook myself from the shocked state and stood up, extending my hand her way.

"I am sorry for my unprofessionalism. My name is Aron. Nice to meet you finally. Neither your best friend or your brother stopped talking about you since you returned from Paris, so I must say I've heard a lot but it's nice to finally put the face next to their description."

She took my hand and squeezed it tightly and some kind of spark went up my hand at her shake.

Her smile never left her face as she spoke.

"Yeah, I can say I've heard a lot about you as well. All good I promise."

We got down to business and I explained what her work would be while she was here.

She nodded her head at my explanation, dropped a few questions but mostly she just listened.

But my mind kept repeating that shock that went through me when we touched.

It was something I had never felt before.

Too soon our "meeting" came to an end.

"Ok. If you have no more questions we can start working." I told her, even though I was in no hurry to see her leave my office.

Once more she graced me with her brilliant smile before she stood up.

"I think I have everything for now. But I will drop by if I have any more questions if that's alright?"

"Yes of course. You can always come in if you have a question."

"Ok. Then see you later sir."

"None of that. Just call me Aron please. We try to be as informal as it gets in our company."

"Ok. Aron it is then."

My name on her lips made my cock twitch in my pants and I had a hard time keeping him in check before he developed a full hard on.

Then she turned around and walked towards the door.

And before I say anything else, you need to know I am an ass man.

And Becky's behind, was picture perfect.

Two round globes that just asked for my hands to touch them.

I was ogling her ass shamelessly when suddenly she turned around.

"Oh, I almost forgot."

Once she faced me, I tried to avert my gaze as fast as possible but judging from her red cheeks I was busted.

But she continued speaking anyway.

"Rachel told me to inform you, she would be taking her time off until after the honeymoons and I quote her: because you took away my maid of honour and will be working my ass double time now."

I laughed at those words, because they were so Rachel style.

"No problem, Becky. Guess we will be seeing each other on a daily basis then."

A huge grin spread across her face before she continued on her way to her office.

And in that minute, it hit me.

Rachel's wedding was 2 months away.

Which meant I was "stuck" with Becky for at least those two months.

Let me put it this way:

I was fucked!

Chapter 5 (Becky's POV)

Ok.

I might have gotten myself into a huge mess.

And there was no way out of it.

When Rachel suggested I would be her replacement until after her honeymoon I agreed gladly, because let's face it, I need a job and something to get my mind off everything that's going on.

But when Rachel described her boss, I had this picture of an old round guy with an always happy face.

Wroooong!

Aron was not old at all, probably just a few years older than me, and ladies, he is one hot male specimen.

Tall with light brown hair that almost looks blond, eyes that are neither brown nor green but something between those colours.

Muscles that even his jeans and a button-down shirt can't hide, and a smile to make a lady drop her panties right away.

Thank God I am not wearing them.

Call it professional deformation.

You see, if I wasn't shooting for lingerie, panty lines were a no go, so I adapted to life without panties.

Today I was glad but cursed myself at the same time for my lack of underwear.

You are probably asking yourself why.

I explained the good side already, but the bad side was, nothing held back my wetness at the sight of Aron's panty dropping smile.

But I wasn't here to date my boss even if he had that role only temporarily.

But there was no place for romance in my life at the moment.

I had to do my job efficiently so I would get a good letter of recommendation and could start building my life towards something normal.

So, I dropped down at my desk and started answering the phone.

Job really wasn't bad and I kind of enjoyed it.

But that dark Adonis of my boss didn't want to leave my thoughts.

I finally managed to get him partly of my mind when suddenly he opened his office door with his trademark grin firmly in place.

Like what the hell is wrong with you man? How can someone be so happy all the time?

I've been in his presence only a few hours, but he keeps that smile firmly in place.

And let me tell you something.

Whoever is so happy all the time, hides demons deep under that exterior.

"Hey Becky. Are you doing fine out here?"

I matched his grin with a small smile.

"Sure, am boss. Thank God I know Rachel like me so it's not hard to find things around here."

Why is he still smiling?

Gaaah his happiness is driving me crazy!

Don't get me wrong.

I am not jealous or anything like that.

But it's just impossible to be happy all the time.

Fine. I might be overreacting. I have known the guy for a few hours only. Maybe he is just having a good day.

"Ok. So, I was wondering if you want to grab lunch with me?"

Now I have a problem.

I was bad at these things.

I never knew when someone was just friendly, and when the person was flirting with me.

But I guess either way would be ok in this situation.

I can't lie.

He was hot and I definitely felt sparks when we touched.

But what I really needed right now was a friend, and from what Rachel has told me Aron was a good friend.

So, to hell with all my doubts.

"Yeah sure. Would love to. Just let me grab my things."

I grabbed my purse, keys and phone and we were on our way.

"So, Becky tell me something about yourself?"

A nervous chuckle escaped me.

I know people believe that anyone in my line of work is a self-absorbed person.

But I never was that way and never will be.

I hated speaking about myself honestly.

"Don't you know enough about me from Rachel and Mason already?"

I kept my voice neutral even though I could feel my nervousness.

"Sure, I know many things, but I want to hear it from you."

Ok. Here goes nothing.

"Ok. So, I grew up here in London, I have an older brother Mason, and you could say Rachel is more like a sister than a friend since we practically grew up together. I finished my business and psychology degree but ended up modelling. It all started in my last year of college when we had a fundraiser, and I had this idea of people making their own designs and we students could show them to everyone on the day of the event. It went amazing and someone saw me and approached me with an idea of becoming a model. One year later my career took off and I was traveling the world, making a name for myself. And the rest is history."

He gave me a kind smile and my frozen walls started melting.

"I can see you love your work. I know a bit about what went down when you ended your career, so I won't continue to poke into a wound. So, another subject. Any pets?"

I laughed at his sudden change of subject.

"Not so fast, mister. What about you? Tell me something about yourself?"

If I wasn't looking, I would miss the way his smile dropped for a moment, but he recovered fast.

In its place a fake smile was showing now.

"Not much to tell Becky. Born and raised in London. Finished my computer and business degree and soon after college started with Code hack."

He made it sound simple and boring but this man in front of me was anything but boring.

"What about your parents?"

And for the first time since I met him, his smile dropped completely.

"Not in the picture. Never were."

With those words and a cold stare aimed in the distance somewhere he picked up his pace and I had to practically run after him.

What the hell just happened?

## Chapter 6 (Aron's POV)

Let me tell you a secret.

I am an idiot.

Yeah, yeah, I know it's not really a secret but don't crush my ego right away, ok?

Everything was perfect until I had to open my mouth and ask Becky about her life.

Like it's not obvious she would ask back the same question, if nothing more, just to be polite.

And so here I am.

Walking ahead of her, pissed as all hell.

Not at her, I am angry with myself.

Because believe it or not, just for once I want to be just me.

Aron McNamara.

Not the owner of Code heck, not the poor guy that his own mother abandoned, not a man with high iq.

Just my usual self.

Like I was a few years ago when I just started building my company. Back then I was just one of many hackers that enjoyed his job.

Don't get me wrong, I still love my job, but not the part with papers.

That's why I hired Rachel in the first place.

She didn't care how much money I had in my account, she didn't try to seduce me or get me in her bed, and honestly, she was overqualified with her intelligence, so I was grateful when she decided to stay in the company as my secretary.

But right now, I had a different issue at hand.

Just as I was thinking about a way to apologize to Becky, a small hand took hold of my elbow.

"Hey. I have no idea what I said but I am sorry that I upset you. Can we rewind the last part of our conversation please?"

It felt like a huge rock was lifted from my shoulders at her words.

I gave her my trademark smile, but somehow for the first time ever, it felt like it was fake.

Which it's kind of was, since it was my farce for so long.

But I wouldn't dwell on it right now.

"Don't worry. You did nothing wrong. It's just my head messing with me."

She gave me a look that told me we would get back to this issue at some point.

But I was just relieved she wouldn't dig right now.

I will find a way to avoid those topics in the future.

We continued to my favorite restaurant in London.

"Vicky's heaven" was just a little bar once upon a time, but with a little help from an anonymous donor she managed to upgrade to a nice restaurant with delicious food.

Vicky was one of my childhood friends, who knew everything about my past.

And I know what's going through your mind right now, and let me tell you, you can delete those thoughts.

What me and Vicky had was always platonic.

She was nothing more than a friend, and since she always tried to set me up with her girlfriends, I'd say we were on the same page.

As we stepped inside my hand ended up on Becky's lower back.

She stiffened for a minute but relaxed just as quickly.

When the girl at the front desk saw us, she gave me a huge smile.

"Hey Aron. Your usual table?"

I returned her smile with a polite one.

"Hey Summer. I need a table for two actually. If you have any by the window it would be amazing."

A scowl appeared on her usually cheerful face, and she gave Becky a onceover.

What the hell?

I looked between them, because honestly, I had no clue what was going on.

Becky lifted her chin proudly and returned the scowl she was receiving from Summer.

"Oh." Was all Summer said before she took out a menu and led us towards a table that was indeed situated by a window.

Once we were seated, she turned around and stomped back to the front desk.

I was still confused about Summer's behavior when suddenly Becky started chuckling next to me, "What?"

She just kept chuckling for a few moments before she turned my way, "You know this right now was the best thing that I've encountered in a long time."

I was still looking at her with an expression best described as: "what the fuck?"

"You see that little scowling thing right there wants you badly. And you don't even notice her!"

"What? Summer? No way. I am a regular customer in this restaurant, and I am sure it's not like that."

"Oh, believe me. I would recognize a territorial jealous woman from miles away. And she was both."

I was thinking about her words when a shadow suddenly fell on our table, "Well, well. I think I need to have my eyes checked ASAP. My best friend actually found himself a woman and he brought her to meet me. I was thinking this day would never come."

I need to ask myself, why in the ever-loving hell did I decide to come here?

"Becky, meet Vicky, one of my oldest friends and sometimes a real nightmare. Vicky, meet Becky, my temporary secretary."

Vicky's eyes were as wide as saucers while Becky was as red as a tomato from holding in her laugh, "Oh, so an office romance. Damn I like it. Hi. I am Vicky. Nice to meet you. And if you need any dirt on this guy, don't hesitate to ask."

Becky couldn't contain her laugh anymore and she started laughing uncontrollably.

I think one way or another, today's lunch will not be forgotten any time soon.

## Chapter 7 (Becky's POV)

I know it's not ladylike to laugh like a maniac, but I can't help it.

Vicky's words keep ringing in my head and each time I look at Aron's face the laughter just comes again.

She actually thought that someone like Aron would fall for a girl like me.

Let's be honest.

My life was in ruins at the moment.

And first of all, I had to learn to love myself again.

This person I've become is just not me.

I wanted to be the easy-going cheerful me again.

And I was shocked once I realized I was all these things right now.

I was happy, laughing out loud, and not thinking about the facts of who might be sitting at the table nearby.

I was just enjoying a simple lunch break with my boss and his friend.

I decided it was time to introduce myself as well.

So, I extended my hand in Vicky's direction before I spoke.

"Hei. My name is Rebecka, but everyone calls me Becky. And Aron really is just my boss. But I will admit, I am flattered that he brought me here today. It's a really lovely place."

Vicky's face transformed into one of pure joy.

"Oh, thank you so much. This restaurant is my baby. I started not long ago, bought it with the money my grandparents left me in a trust fund, and opened a bar. It was used for that purpose for many years, but suddenly an anonymous donor contacted me with a huge amount of money and support if I wanted to upgrade to a restaurant. I was skeptical at first because all he wanted was for one dish to be on the menu every day and a special brand of beer on tap. And that's it. I thought there must be some secret behind it, but up until today, no secret was revealed to me. So, I just hope it stays that way."

When she spoke about her restaurant, she was practically glowing.

But what captured my attention the most was those demands of her anonymous donor.

So, I asked about it.

"What kind of food and beer did he demand to be available?"

She chuckled and pointed a finger in Aron's direction.

"He wanted lasagna and the dark beer on tap that was not doing so well, and we wanted to replace it. And those are the only things that Aron ever eats and drinks here. If I didn't know any better, I would suspect him, but he knows if he ever offers me that amount of money, I will break his arms. "

I was just about to say that it might still be him when he suddenly kicked my leg under the table.

I looked at him accordingly, but he just gave me a mischievous smile.

Damn him and his dimples.

But if he wanted to play games, we could play.

I smirked his way before I turned my attention back to Vicky.

"You know, if you have any dirt on this guy, it will really come in handy. Especially if I want to get him into my bed shortly."

At the same moment, two things happened.

Aron stiffened beside and Vicky started jumping up and down while she was clapping her hands like a child.

"Give me five minutes. I will bring you guys dark beer on the house, and then Aron can pray for the ground to swallow him, and you my dear friend will get all the dirt you want."

I laughed at her quickly retrieving form.

She really was something else...

"What the hell Becky? I hope you were joking because I can't afford to have a secretary that wants to seduce me."

I looked at him with an evil smirk on my face.

"You know I would gladly tell you if it was a joke or not, but it seems that you like to keep secrets, especially from your friends so I guess I won't tell you anything."

He was starting to get nervous, and it was pretty much obvious by just looking at his face.

"What do you mean by that? I don't keep any secrets."

"Really? So why does Vicky still have no clue that you are the anonymous donor?"

I could see he wanted to deny it, but I just gave him a stern look and his shoulders dropped.

"You've heard what she said Becky. She would break my arm if she knew I gave her that money. I just wanted to help her, as she helped me when I was younger. I was a boy that got into trouble at every turn, but Vicky took me under her wing and made sure I was staying out of trouble. It is probably thanks to her that I am where I am today and not rotting in prison."

His words touched me and melted another piece of my frozen heart.

I could see he really cared about her and that's something that you just don't make fun of, "I was kidding Aron. I just want to be a good replacement for Rachel while she plans her dream wedding."

He gave me a kind smile and suddenly grabbed my hand.

He brought it to his lips and gave a gentle kiss.

This man will be the death of me.

"Thank you so much for your honesty. I swear I was freaking out there for a second."

Ouch. Now those were the words no woman ever wanted to hear.

"Why? Am I that ugly?"

His smile dropped and was replaced with shock in seconds.

"Fuck! No Becky. It's nothing like that. You are beautiful and any man that says differently is either an asshole or lying. Or maybe even both. But I just don't have time for any kind of romance in my life right now. Or either a desire for it."

Now that sounded a bit better for my bruised ego.

"It's ok. But Vicky is coming back so prepare to suffer."

A painful groan escaped him, but his trademark smile was back in its place. So, I guess we were back to normal.

Now if I could only get rid of the butterflies in my stomach each time, he smiled at me.

Does alcohol drown them?

Let's hope so.

Cheers.

## Chapter 8 (Aron's POV)

Surprisingly lunch wasn't as painful as I thought.

They tortured me with all kinds of embarrassing memories from my early years, but it was fun. Even if that fun was at my expense.

Now I was sitting in my office again but couldn't get the beauty that was sitting in front of it out of my head.

All I could think about ever since we returned from lunch, was how her hand accidentally brushed against mine from time to time. How our knees were touching all the time.

How her laugh made me feel lighter and happier than I was in years.

How her eyes sparkled with mischief when she was taunting me with the knowledge of my little secret.

She really was something special.

And I was starting to get scared of that fact.

Because if I wouldn't trade my way around her carefully, I could easily fall for her.

Hard and fast.

And love or falling for someone was something that simply wasn't in my cards.

When you love someone, they leave you.

So, it's better to keep everyone within arm's reach and keep up my cheerful mask.

That way no one can leave me, and no one can hurt me.

Do you remember how I told you that I needed a dog?

Well, maybe I don't need it.

But I would still get one. He or she can be my best friend and my companion, so I won't feel so alone.

But what I really needed right now, was to get laid.

Because it was starting to be as clear as the sky on a sunny day.

I was horny!

There was no unusual attraction between me and Becky.

I was just horny, so my mind started coming up with ideas to get her into my bed.

Well, this time it will be a no-go.

So, the only other option I had was to go out and find someone.

In a few moments I had a plan put together.

I picked up my phone and dialed one of my best employees and best friends.

"Hey boss man, how can I help you?"

"Hey Mason. I've told you a thousand times to stop calling me that but instead of stopping you taught Rachel to call me that as well. I have no idea why I still count you as one of my best friends."

Even though those words were said as seriously as possible we both knew I was kind of joking, and we also knew Mason won't stop calling me boss man.

Why was I even trying at this point?

My thoughts were proved correctly when I heard his chuckle.

"Now, now. Don't get angry, boss man. It doesn't suit you. And you can also get wrinkles. And to answer your questions. First of all, I am one of your best programmers, I was by your side when Code hack almost went to hell. We saved each other's asses countless times, and I need to repay my debt. You know when you made me realize I was an asshole."

It was my time to chuckle at his words. I knew exactly what opportunity he was referring to, but I couldn't pass up a chance to tease him a little.

"Which time exactly are we talking about? You know it happened many times that someone had to remind you, you're an asshole."

"Hardy-ha-ha. Now down to business. What do you need?"

"I know you are deep into this wedding planning, but I was wondering if you'd have time for a friend to go out together. Grab some drinks or something like that?"

"You, my dear friend, are a lifesaver. Just tell me when and where and I'll be there."

We decided to meet at Vicky's restaurant around 7, which gave me enough time to go home and take a shower before meeting with Mason.

When I walked out of my office, Becky's desk was empty, which meant she had already left.

I felt both relieved and disappointed, but I pushed down this other side of me and focused on the relief.

It was better this way.

The less I saw her, the less possibilities for me to fall for her.

No!

Scratch that!

That was not a possibility at all. End of discussion.

I went home and got ready.

I was at Vicky's restaurant a few minutes too early, but it seems like Mason was used to this, because he was already waiting for me.

We went inside and straight to the bar.

We ordered our usual beer brew, and some French fries to soak the alcohol in our system.

"So, tell me. How is my sister doing? I hope you don't have any problems with her?"

"Nah man. Don't worry. She does her job perfectly and that's the only thing that matters."

Just when he was about to reply his phone rang.

He pulled it out and I knew right away it was Rachel because his whole face lit up.

"Hey sweetheart. Yeah, we are at Vicky's. Sure, why not? Ok. I will be waiting. Love you too."

I looked at Mason with a raised eyebrow as soon as he finished his call.

"Sorry boss man. I guess I will have to cut our man night short. Rachel is coming so I can take her home. She has those sickness periods again."

"Don't they call it morning sickness?"

Mason's eyebrows shoot upwards in disbelief.

"Right? Why would you call it that if it comes at any time of the day!"

We kept on chatting while Mason waited for Rachel.

It was good to have a few hours with him even if he cut our night short.

After all, I couldn't be happier for him.

He got himself a good woman, was getting ready to get married and was expecting a kid.

What more could a man ask for?

Suddenly he stood up.

"They are here. See you tomorrow at the office boss man."

They?

Just when I was about to ask him about it, a female body stepped in front of me.

"Hey. I hope you don't mind if I replace Mason for a few drinks?"

I lifted my head only to be met with those blue sapphires I was trying to forget in all the alcohol.

"Nah. Be my guest. What would you like to drink tonight, Becky?"

"Hmm. Whiskey on rocks sounds good."

If she doesn't get her drink fast, I am sure I had another thing which was right now as hard as rocks.

## Chapter 9 (Becky's POV)

We were just hanging around with Rachel in the bar next door to Code hack.

I had already had a few drinks in while Rachel was drinking her soda.

She told me about her pregnancy only yesterday!

I mean come on! We were best friends!

So, I was still a bit hurt, but not too much.

I still accepted her offer for drinks.

After all, I still loved my best friend.

She was like a sister I never had.

So, staying mad at her for long was not an option.

As I was saying, we were just chatting away, when she suddenly became unnaturally pale.

"Rach, are you ok?"

"Sure. It's just this morning sickness. It's a nasty thing. And no, I have no idea why they call it morning sickness if it hits you at any time of the day."

I chuckled at her rambling, but quickly called over our bartender to pay our bill.

As we were already walking down the street, she called Mason to let him know she was coming to him, so he could take her home.

I knew Mason was out with friends, but I had no idea with whom.

After all, I didn't make it a habit to hang around with him and his friends.

As we approached our destination, I realized we were standing in front of Vicky's restaurant, so I didn't have to guess long to know who was inside with Mason.

"Becky I am so sorry I had to cut short our girls' night. But since I am dragging Mason away, you could stay and have a drink or two with Aron you know."

Aaaand if I had any doubts about my suspicions before, they are gone now.

But right now, I couldn't find anything wrong with me hanging around with Aron.

So, I did what any responsible adult with some common sense would do.

I accepted her idea with arms wide open.

Somewhere in my subconscious I knew I would regret my decision in the morning but right now, I couldn't find it in me to give a fuck.

So, I walked inside Vicky's restaurant like I owned the place, and I could hear Rachel chuckling behind me.

I know I was acting like a spoiled diva, which I never was, but I really didn't care.

I waved at my brother, and he stood right away.

He passed me by with a kiss on my cheek and a thank you.

As I stepped in front of Aron, I could see confusion clearly written all over his face.

But when he lifted his head to meet my eyes and gave me his honest dimpled smile, I was a goner.

"Hey. I hope you don't mind if I replace Mason for a few drinks?"

"Nah. Be my guest. What would you like to drink tonight, Becky?"

"Hmm. Whiskey on rocks sounds good."

Even in a crowded bar area I could hear him gulp audibly.

"A woman after my heart."

I chuckled because I knew he didn't mean it as many women would take his words.

It simply meant he preferred the same choice of drinks.

No hidden meaning.

"Then I guess your heart is as jaded as mine is."

He gave me a funny look.

"Now why would a girl as pretty and as successful as you be jaded?"

A sad smile crossed my lips. He was right. I was kind of successful in my line of work, but that didn't mean I was happy.

"Sometimes I just want my life to be simple. Sure, it's easier now, but for how long? I kind of got used to being watched all the time, but that doesn't mean I like it. I thought I loved my line of work, but recently realized it was the complete opposite. In fact, I hate it! Watching what you eat, where you go, who you hang around with... I'd rather have a boring life honestly."

I was expecting to see pity in his eyes, but instead there was understanding.

"I know what you mean. It's not as difficult for me as it is for you, since I am not a model but still at the start there were so many journalists just digging for dirt in my life, just because I made it at a young age. And they almost managed to ruin me and my reputation by leaking false facts but thank God I had Mason by my side at that point already. And together we managed to rise from the ashes metaphorically saying."

I remembered that time he was talking about.

Mason was stressed at that time because he was trying to find a code that would help him keep those rumors away from the public eye and after months of hard work and brainstorming, he managed to accomplish his goal.

After that they started basically from the ground and build up the company as it was today

Every person had to go through a thorough check before even getting a chance to interview at Code hack.

I was probably an exception because I was Mason's sister.

Or was I?

"Aron. Can I ask you something? I know you check everyone that applies for a job position in your company. So, I was wondering, did you check me as well?"

An adorable blush crept across his face.

"Well, I didn't at first because it was a sudden decision, but I did later in the afternoon. I hope you won't get mad, it's just for the safety of Code hack."

I chuckled. It was just as I was suspecting. He was a control freak. But after what he's been through, I couldn't really blame him. I guess it was true what they said. You could never be too careful.

"Don't sweat it. I understand it was a necessary evil. But I do wonder if there was anything interesting?"

If he could get any redder, he would change into a tomato.

"Nope. Nothing interesting."

I squinted my eyes at him. It was evident he was lying. But what could it be? Wait. No. It couldn't be!

"You found my photos from the job application!"

I was horrified just thinking about it.

Those pictures were not one of my best ones.

The job application stated they wanted a lingerie model, so I used what I had at hand at that point.

Which meant I used my sexiest lingerie, which was nowhere close to professional.

It was a black set of thongs and a lacy bra.

Nothing special or professional, but it left little to imagination.

"I...might have yes. But I swear I closed it as fast as I opened it."

That did bring me some relief, but I was still embarrassed.

So, I changed the topic fast.

We were talking about nothing really but still it felt nice.

And soon a nice buzz from the alcohol washed over me.

Now my brain was starting to function only on lust, and I knew I was fucked...

## Chapter 10 (Aron's POV)

You know things will go wrong once you start noticing all the sexy details about your best friend's sister.

Well let's be honest here.

I found those details sexy the moment I met Becky in person.

But right now, with my brain soaked in beer and whiskey I was moment away from acting on my lust induced ideas.

All I wanted was for us to be alone somewhere and get to the fun part.

Hopefully I will get her out of my system as well.

Somewhere in the back of my mind I heard a voice telling me that we would still need to work together for at least a few moments, but I was willing to put that part on mute for now and deal with it in the morning.

And it wasn't just lust speaking right now either.

I genuinely liked her company.

She was funny and smart, she was a good listener that actually listened to what I was telling her, even when I spoke about my work.

"So, are we ready to call it a night?"

Her words brought me back from my thoughts.

I looked around and realized the bar area was almost empty, which could only mean that Vicky was already closing down.

And when I looked at my watch the time indeed shocked me.

It was already 2 am.

I couldn't even remember when the last time was, I stayed out this long.

"Yeah sure. Let me just pay our tab and I will walk you home."

"You don't need to do any of those things. I can pay for my half and call a cab you know."

At her words a sense of protectiveness washed over me.

A cab in the middle of the night, in London?

I don't think so!

No way was I letting her do things her way.

But what I knew about Becky so far, showed me that she was a very proud kind of woman.

So, no way would I be telling her things the way I thought them in my head.

"Now what kind of a gentleman would I be if I let you pay for your drinks while you were just being good company to my sorry ass? Also taking a cab alone in the middle of the night is not really a safe option."

When she narrowed her eyes at me, I knew she misunderstood me.

"I didn't mean it for a woman Becky, so you can put your hackles away. It's not a safe option for anyone. Not me, not you. So now that we have got things settled, I will get our tab settled and we will enjoy each other's company for a little while longer while I escort you to your house, ok?"

What I didn't mention was that we were heading in the same direction anyway.

My house was just a few blocks away from hers, so I wouldn't have a long way to get home once I dropped her at her house.

I paid our tab and was just waiting for Becky to collect all her things when suddenly my phone started vibrating in my pocket.

I almost ignored it, but at the last moment changed my mind, and thank God I did because it was Aunt Liz calling me.

I answered immediately because if she was calling me at this hour, something would be wrong. Very wrong.

"What's wrong aunt Liz?"

"Aron, don't come home tonight. Your mother came around looking for you. I've told her some lies to get her to leave but I have a bad feeling. If she came looking for you, she found out about you and your company. She wants something from you."

Cold shivers ran down my back at her words. If my biological mother was in town, I had no doubt Aunt Liz guessed correctly. She wanted something from me.

"No worries aunt. I will go to my friend's house tonight, and we can meet in the morning for coffee so we can discuss what to do ok?"

We said a fast goodbye and just when I was about to put my phone away a hand wrapped around my lower arm.

"Hey. Are you ok? You look like you've seen a ghost."

A dark chuckle escaped me. She was almost right. Except I didn't see her, just heard about her. The funny part was, even if I saw my biological mother pass me by on the street, I doubted I'd recognize her. I've never even seen the woman in person.

"Yeah. I am fine. But I do have a weird question for you."

She narrowed her eyes at me once again and I couldn't help it but find her adorable when she looked at me like that.

"Shoot."

I took a deep breath before speaking. What I was about to ask her wasn't easy for me, but I couldn't think of any other option. I mean who in their right mind is up at 2 am?

"I would need a place to crash tonight. I was on the phone with Aunt Liz, and something came up, so she called me not to come home."

She looked at me suspiciously.

"Ok but I have one condition."

A weird sense of dread washed over me, because I could already assume what that condition would be.

But funny fact time, I didn't feel any fear or reluctance. Well not the way I usually felt when someone asked me about my past.

"You need to tell me about this thing or person that came up, so I know what I am dealing with. Deal?"

She extended her hand towards me, and I hesitated for only a moment before I shook it and sealed the deal.

Strangely for the first time, I felt relief at the thought of telling someone about my past and my parents.

"Deal. Now let's get to your house."

Chapter 11 (Becky's POV)

After we came back, I made us some tea and set it all in the living room.

But looking at Aron, you could tell he wasn't psychically present.

He might be standing in the same room as I was, but his mind was somewhere far away.

And that scared me very much.

Because once a person got that far away look in their eyes it could mean only two things.

Either they were thinking about something really nice, or something really awful.

And since Aron asked for a place to crash, I'd say it was the latter.

The suspense was killing me, but I didn't dare utter a word, so I was just waiting patiently.

Who am I kidding?

There wasn't a patient bone in my body.

After a few long minutes that felt like ages had passed he finally spoke.

But his voice was dull and void of any emotions.

"You see, once upon a time, I thought my life was perfect. But as I got older, I started noticing there were little differences between me and my aunt, whom at that time I thought was my mother. There were also many differences between me and my cousin Ana. But first I thought I probably just took after my father. Sadly, that was not the case. One day a letter arrived. But the thing that confused me was that it was supposed to be sent by my mother. So as a confused teenager I started asking questions. Aunt answered every one of them with pain in her eyes. She loved her sister, but she also told me she was not a good person. The final straw for my aunt was the day she found me on her doorsteps only a week after I was born. She gave me the letter that was left by my side when she abandoned me. I opened it and you know what it said? That no guy in their right mind would financially support her and a baby and since she didn't have anything valuable to gain from having me, she would leave me at my aunts.  Now I have no idea how a heart can break for someone whom you didn't even know, but at that moment my heart broke anyway. Because as soon as I was born, I was a burden to someone."

He was lost in those painful memories, and it was all too much to bear for me, so I stood up and moved next to him, putting my hand on his arm to show him my support.

He gave me a gentle smile that was far from his trademark smirk I saw so often in the past few hours I knew him.

This one was genuine and made him look stunning.

He put one hand over mine before he continued.

"After I discovered the truth, I was angry at the world for some time. That's when I met Vicky and she beat some sense back into my stubborn ass. She made me realize that I had nothing to complain about. Sure. My mother abandoned me. But not because there was something wrong with me. She did it for selfish reasons. And at the end of the day, I had an aunt that loved and raised me as if I was her own child. There were never any differences between me and her daughter. So, I apologized to my aunt, and I make sure to tell or show her every day how much she means to me. In my eyes she is my mother. She raised me, fed me, made sure I didn't give up on myself and believed in me when no one else did. Practically I owe her everything. And remember that time when my company almost fell apart, and Mason helped me? Well, me and my aunt and her daughter Ana think it was my mother's doing. Since she couldn't get a piece of the cake, she would destroy it. I had no proof of it, so I just focused on rebuilding my company. But tonight, as we were about to leave Vicky's place, my aunt called me. My mother is back in town. She is looking for me. And that can only mean one thing. She found out I changed my surname and built a future for myself. And now she wants something from me. As if I owe her anything."

I was a temperamental person by nature, but what I was feeling right now was beyond anything I ever felt before.

"Are you shitting me? That bitch! How dare she? First, she abandons an innocent baby to fend for themselves. What if your aunt wasn't such an amazing person with a heart of gold? And now she wants something from you? She dares show her face in the same town as you live in. I swear if I ever meet her, I have some really nice things to tell her. Also, a slap or two would do her good!"

I took a deep breath and realized Aron was staring at me with eyes wide open.

A blush crept over my cheeks at his intense stare.

I guess I overstepped the boundaries.

"I am so..."

My words were cut off when his lips crashed to mine.

I was stunned for a moment.

What the hell?

But after a moment I started kissing him back.

And oh my gosh what a kiss it was.

It was the kind of kiss that curled your toes and made your heartbeat faster.

I clung to his shirt for my dear life.

His hands were cupping my face while his lips devoured me like I was the most delicious dessert in the world.

A moan escaped me and suddenly I felt my back hitting a wall.

When did we move?

Never mind, back to business.

His hands roamed all over my upper body, but never where I needed his touch.

My hands explored his body thoroughly as well.

Suddenly he dipped lower and put his hands under my ass to lift me up.

My legs instinctively went around his hips, and he pressed his hardness into my wanting aching core.

I gasped at the contact.

Suddenly he moved away from my lips but still kept us in the same position.

I looked at his eyes, surprised to find him smiling down at me.

"Not once did anyone get so defensive on my account. And let me tell you sweetheart. It's a pure turn on."

A blush once again spread across my cheeks.

"What you went through is just so fucking awful! She doesn't deserve anything you built with your own hands!"

His smile grew even wider.

"I knew there was something special about you from the moment you stepped into my office. I also knew I would have a hard time keeping my hands to myself. But I had no idea how perfect you are for me."

He didn't even give me a chance to reply, before his lips were back on mine.

And I was lost.

I was drowning in everything that was Aron.

Consequences be damned.

I will deal with everything in the morning.

For now, I just wanted to enjoy all the attention this Adonis was giving me.

Tomorrow morning, I will return to real life.

Tomorrow.

Chapter 12 (Aron's POV)

I had her pinned against the wall in seconds.

And if I was used to having women let me lead the way, let me tell you, Becky was not one of them.

She gave as good as she got.

My hands didn't want to be on the nice side either.

They were all over her.

I could hear a small voice in my head telling me to stop, that it was not a good idea, but right now, I couldn't care less.

This woman was perfect in every way possible.

From the way she got everything done with determination and passion, to the way she handled her practically destroyed career as a model. And last but not least, the way she defended me, even though she didn't know me for long.

The way she got mad at my biological mother was something I never experienced from another person.

Those few that knew the story usually gave me a look full of pity, but in her eyes, I could only detach rage and understanding.

And I have no idea why, but it was a turn on for me.

All the consumed alcohol probably had something to do with it as well.

I doubt I would even be ready to tell her the whole story otherwise.

But right now, I had no time to dwell on those things, because there was a gorgeous woman in my hands.

And it looked like she was aching for me as much as I was for her.

I started trailing kisses all over her neck and down to her collar bone.

She was a moaning mess by now already, and each time I gave her a light bite her breath hitched.

Hmm, so she likes it a bit on the rough side.

Time to test that theory.

I put my hands under her ass and lifted her so now her wet middle was pressing right at my hard member.

Damn it, but if we didn't get to the action soon, I would come like a teenager when losing his virginity.

So, I sat down on the couch with her firmly planted on my lap.

First, I had to get rid of her T-shirt, so let's get to it.

As eager as I was to get her naked, I was surprised my hands didn't shake.

So, I managed to get rid of her shirt in record time.

And what awaited me there was pure perfection.

A simple red lacy bra with a small bow in the middle.

The lace was so thin I could see her nipples through it, but it was most definitely not enough for me.

So, I pushed one of her cups down so I could have free access.

As soon as I managed to remove the offending lace, I sucked on her nipple hard while my hand pinched the other one.

And a pure moan of pleasure escaped from Becky's mouth.

So, I had my answer.

She liked a bit of pain.

I continued sucking and pinching, only pausing for moments when switching to the other side.

I loved her sweet moans and whimpers.

They were perfect indicators of me doing something right.

I was so into her tits that it took me quite some time to realize she was grinding herself against my hardness.

The pressure was just enough to start building my pleasure.

"Yes, Aron yes. Just like that."

I could feel she was close by the way she was clutching my shoulders.

And there was no other goal in my mind but to make her reach that peak.

I sucked on her nipple harder and bit it lightly for good measure and it was enough for the firecracker in my arms.

What I didn't realize was how close she got me to my own release.

Just when I was about to enjoy her afterglow she pressed on my member one final time, harder than she did before.

And my world exploded. She was limp in my arms and there was a huge wet spot on my pants. Great. Now I have nothing to wear.

"You have some sweats in Mason's room. He left them behind when he moved in with Rachel."

It was like she was reading my mind. A soft chuckle escaped me and subconsciously I dropped a kiss on her head.

She stiffened in my arms immediately and as not to make it any weirder I stood up with her still in my arms.

"Ok princess but first we need to get you to your bed."

As a response she just cuddled closer to me, so I took that as a yes.

I put her on her bed, and she was out as the light in a few moments.

So, I went to get myself a pair of pants and was just about to put them on when my brain went into overdrive again.

Did she want me to sleep in her bed?

Probably not.

The hint about Mason's pants was probably a subtle way to tell me I was sleeping in Mason's room.

Now that my mind was made I climbed into bed as well.

It was nearing morning and I had to get some sleep.

Tomorrow, I had to come up with a plan to get rid of my biological mother.

And this time I had to get her out of it for good.

Easier said than done when the woman in question understands only the language of money.

Sure, I had a lot of money but that didn't mean I was throwing it around.

And definitely not on a woman that never gave me anything except gave birth to me. And she thought she could just waltz back in my life and demand her share of it.

Not going to happen.

The end of the story. But I would make those things a reality in the morning. Right now, as I said, I needed sleep.

And if I get to dream about the beauty in the room next to mine, I wouldn't mind. Not at all.

## Chapter 13 (Becky's POV)

I woke up with a massive headache.

Alone! In my bed.

Now if I wasn't really really drunk, there would be no chances that I was hallucinating.

Yet I could swear there was a gorgeous boss with me yesterday.

I could also remember I dry humped him until I found my release.

But then I can barely remember anything after that.

Especially not how I got to my own bed, or where he was right now, because the other side of my bed was cold.

But I think it's best I go hunt down some pain killers first.

Then I can maybe think when the little man inside my head won't try to break my skull.

I went to the kitchen, found some pain killers and orange juice and decided to prepare some breakfast.

Food was always good to soak up alcohol, or a hangover in my case.

And since Aron drank as much as I did or maybe even more, I guess he won't be opposed to some food as well.

I took out some toast, cheese and bacon and started making breakfast.

Since I am not a model anymore, at least not officially, I don't have to watch my food input.

So, some toast with melted cheese and some crusty bacon sounds amazing.

I was so absorbed in my work that I didn't hear Aron come into the kitchen until he was right behind me leaning over my shoulder and trying to peek at what I was preparing.

"Morning, beautiful."

His voice brought me back from my thoughts and scared me at the same time, so a small scream escaped my lips while my head bumped his chin.

"Damn you scared me! How can you walk so silently when you are such a giant?"

I turned around only to realize my mistake.

He was standing there in nothing else but a pair of tight-fitting boxers.

Forget the food. I want him for my breakfast.

He was rubbing his chin while he chuckled.

"I wasn't silent at all. I even bumped my knee on my way to the kitchen because I rarely sleep anywhere else but at my house. So, since I am used to my layout of the furniture, I manage usually to go around even half asleep, but when I woke up, I didn't realize I was in your house so I bumped my knee while trying to sleep and walk to get myself something to drink and some pain killers."

This time it was my turn to chuckle.

He looked so adorable right now with a small pout on his lips, like I should feel sorry for him because he bumped his knee.

Suddenly his eyes went lower down my body and too late I realized his presence turned me on and I was only in my T-shirt that I put on when I woke up and a pair of really short shorts. And no bra.

So now my nipples were saying hi to Aron as well.

A devilish smirk spread across his face while his eyes found their way to mine.

He took a step closer while I automatically took one step back.

But I had nowhere to run since my back hit the counter already.

"You like what you see, princess?"

I didn't dare open my mouth, because I knew the truth would spill out so instead, I only glared at him.

But he wasn't fazed at all.

Instead, he took another step closer and now he was only a breath away, his arms caging me in on both sides.

"You know, I think we finished too fast yesterday. So, we should really repeat that and make it last a bit longer."

I had no time to argue or agree with him because his mouth was on mine in a second.

His hands went under my ass, and I was sitting on the counter in moments, my legs wrapped around his waist.

I couldn't deny it.

The tension and sparks between us were like something out of a fairytale.

And no matter how passionate our kiss was, I wanted more.

So, my hands began roaming around his shoulders, down to his amazing, sculpted abs and that mouthwatering six packs that I just realized were actually eight packs.

Damn it! Where was this man hiding all my life?

Even if I didn't do relationships at the moment, I would appreciate a strong handsome male and his attention right now.

I was just about to pull down his boxers while his hands were all over my breasts squeezing and making me a moaning mess, when suddenly his phone started ringing on the counter next to us.

The sound was so unexpected it made me jump.

Aron on the other hand didn't seem fazed by it at all.

"Just ignore it. I will call them back later."

His words were murmured against my neck while he trailed his kiss along it and down lower.

Just when he reached for the hem of my T-shirt his phone went off again.

"Who the fuck is so persistent!"

His eyes were blazing with rage until he took his phone and saw the caller's ID.

"Hey aunty. Yeah, I managed. No, I will be there in 30. Ok. Love you too."

He disconnected the call and gave me a look that told me just how much he wanted to continue what we started.

"Don't worry Aron. You have things to take care of. I understand. And you need to keep that harpy out of your life."

Ha gave me a grateful smile and moved back between my legs.

"Can I come back in the evening? We can go out to have dinner and later we can continue what we started?"

His hands were running up and down my thighs and he was fraying every last ounce of common sense in my brain.

So, I gave him a smile and an answer I didn't expect from myself.

"I'd love to. But I can cook so we can stay inside?"

"Perfect. I will be here around 7."

He gave me one last peck and went out the door.

And now I was sitting on the counter, thinking about the mess I just made.

I didn't mind us continuing what we started.

Not at all.

And even though it sounded like a date, the thought made my heart race, but in a good way, which was weird, but we will come back to that later.

But what was bugging me was the fact that I had to cook us dinner because of my long tongue now.

Want to know what part of that bugged me?

I COULDN'T COOK!

So now I was fucked.

I quickly pulled out my phone and dialed the only person that could help me and wouldn't judge me.

She picked up on the second ring.

And I didn't even give her a chance to greet me.

"Rachel, I need help and I need it asap!"

The only answer I got before she disconnected the call, "On my way. Make coffee."

Thank God for best friends.

## Chapter 14 (Aron's POV)

I was on cloud number nine honestly.

I can't even believe she agreed to go out with me.

Well technically we won't be going out at all, but that's fine with me.

I can get her out of her clothes even faster in that scenario.

I'll be honest. I had no idea when the last time was, I even had such an interest in a woman.

But Becky just seems to ignite a fire inside of me and she is the only one that can put it down.

And I know it's all going fast since we knew each other for only a day, but since Mason and Rachel always spoke about her it kind of felt like I knew her all my life already.

I knew pretty much everything a man can know about a woman. So, I wasn't really worried about anything.

After all she also said when we were at Vicky's yesterday, that she wasn't looking for anything serious. At least not until she finds her footing again.

Which is completely logical since she lost everything in one day.

Well not everything, but it was written in her eyes how much modelling meant to her.

I still had no clue about the background of that story.

Guess I'll have to ask her tonight.

I knew only what I read in the newspapers, and we all know there is rarely written the complete truth.

But I had to get my mind back on track right now.

I just stepped in front of the little cafe where I would meet my aunt.

I had no time to think about a plan of action against my mother, but I hope we can come up with something together.

When I entered, I saw my aunt sitting in the back right away. She gave me a huge smile and a wave.

I returned the smile and walked over to her table, "Hey auntie. I hope you managed to get some sleep."

"Oh, don't worry about me sweetheart. I am more worried about you. Did you manage to get any sleep? And how did I even manage to catch you while you were still up? It was past midnight, and I was sure you would be asleep already."

I could feel a blush starting to form on my face and my aunt wasn't blind, so she narrowed her eyes right away, "Spill it young man!"

I chuckled before I told her all about Becky. There was a spark in her eyes that became brighter with every word I spoke.

"My dear Aron. Just from listening to you I can tell you like her already. And honestly, she doesn't sound like a bad woman. So why would you want to just spend some time with her and not think about a future together?"

Once again, my aunt was aiming straight for the finish line.

What was weird was that thoughts about the future together didn't even scare me, "Aunt, it's a bit early to speak about things like the future together. Let's take it slowly. What do you say?"

She frowned but still agreed, "Fine. Let it be your way. But my boy you are not getting any younger. And neither am I so please think about that. I want grandchildren someday and you know that!"

It was time I pulled her back to the topic that needed our attention, "Ok auntie. I will keep that in mind. But tell me now, what did that woman want from you again?"

A heavy sigh escaped her lips before she gave me an answer, "If I would believe her words then she just wants to get to know you, but since we both know better, I would say she wants your money. She even knew we changed your last name. So, I guess she is probably close with someone you know. But right now, we need to find a way to keep her far away from you."

Her words made me think hard about what she said. Someone I knew. But who could that be? No one knew my history or my mother, "I will think of something auntie. Now tell me how are you and how is Ana? Got a new boyfriend already?"

"Oh, that daughter of mine will be the death of me I swear. A few days ago, she called me and told me she would become a lesbian because every man is a useless man whore. Can you believe her?"

My coffee went down the wrong way and I started coughing and laughing at the same time.

Damn I miss that little spitfire. She always kept her mom on her toes. But she loved her like no one else ever could. Even though sometimes she gave her a minor heart-attack. I had to arrange dinner with those two in the near future. I miss them both.

And since Ana was in Manchester studying, we didn't get to see each other often, "Ana has her holidays in a few days. We should get together for dinner at my place. What do you say?"

She gave me a megawatt smile and agreed right away.

Now if only this day would stay as good as it started, I wouldn't mind at all. But we all know that all good things come to an end.

Don't we?

## Chapter 15 (Becky's POV)

I was a nervous wreck.

Biting my nails and walking aimlessly around my house while I waited for Rachel to arrive.

I had to make a perfect dinner.

I have no idea why it meant so much to me, but it did.

Also, I knew my best friend.

As soon as I tell her what kind of help, I need she will be drilling for information about the reasons behind my need to learn how to cook.

I was never good at it.

And let's be honest.

As a model I didn't really eat much, and I had enough money to eat in different restaurants each time.

I am not bragging but that's the kind of lifestyle I was used to.

But now, I guess it was time for me to step down from my pedestal and learn things that any normal person at my age knew how to do.

Like cooking.

Finally, my bell rang, and I practically ran to my door. Rachel pulled me into a hug as soon as I opened the door, "Don't worry Becky. I will help you hide the body."

I burst into laughter, "What body? What are you talking about?"

She gave me her evil smile before answering my question, "Well, you spoke with such urgency I was sure we had to dig a grave and hide someone's body."

At her words we both burst into another fit of laughter.

Damn I loved this woman.

She knew exactly how to calm down my nerves.

I pulled her inside and closed the door behind her.

"We don't have a body to hide. Yet. But if you don't help me, we just might have it in the evening. I need you to help me make dinner for two. And we only have until 6pm because I need to get ready as well."

Her face practically started glowing at my words.

"You naughty woman! Who are we making dinner for? Spill it all or I won't help you out!"

Told you.

"Ok. But you need to promise not to tell Mason anything about it. Do we have a deal?"

She looked troubled for a moment.

"You know I hate lying to him. But ok. I guess I can keep one thing from him. Now tell me. Who is your mystery man?"

I took a deep breath and told my best friend the truth.

"Aron. He is coming over for dinner tonight, and maybe to stay another night."

Her face fell and was filled with concern in seconds.

"Another night? Becky, you came back only yesterday. I have nothing against Aron, but I know he is not one for relationships."

I looked at her with a little bit of anger since I could hear judgment in her voice.

"I am a grown ass woman Rachel. And yes, I only came back yesterday. But we kind of clicked. And he needed a place to stay yesterday so I helped him out. It might have gotten a little steamy, but we slept in separate rooms and beds. And who was talking about a relationship? I've told you I need to first find myself before approaching those subjects. And I expected more support from you. But here you are judging me."

Her face became sad at my words. I know I hurt her, but I wanted her to feel the same I did at her words.

"I am sorry. I should support you; you are right. I just don't want to see you get hurt. I hope you know that. I love you, Becky. Never forget that."

I know she was just looking out for me. But it still hurts.

It reminded me of all the bad choices I made in the past when it came to male population.

"I know Rach. Now will you help me please? I don't want to poison the poor man."

A giggle escaped her, and she engulfed me in one of her trademark hugs.

We never managed to stay angry at one another for long.

We went to the kitchen and Rachel helped me prepare everything for dinner.

Since we didn't have much time left, we decided on spaghetti Bolognese.

Simple and fast but delicious.

She showed me how you can tell pasta is cooked just right and helped me prepare the sauce.

Once we were finished the whole house smelled amazing and I couldn't wait to see Aron's expression when he tasted my dinner.

Rachel made herself comfortable in my living room with a glass of red wine, which the doctor didn't forbid, and I ran upstairs to get ready.

I just stepped out of the shower when I could hear my doorbell.

"I will get that so you can get dressed!"

I know my best friend's words should make me feel better, but it just made me more nervous.

And I started running around my room, looking for clothes because the words that were repeating in my head were not good.

Those words sounded like this:

Oh shit!

I knew Rachel and looking back at her expression and words when I told her who my dinner companion was, I would say she would be grilling him right now.

I found clothes in a record time and didn't even care that I was make-up free and wearing a T-shirt and jeans.

It will have to be good enough.

I almost tripped over my own feet a few times on my way downstairs.

When I was a step away from the living room, I could hear Rachel's next question and it made me pause. I wanted to hear the answer as well.

"What are your intentions with Becky, Aron? You know she's been through a lot in the past year."

I could hear a deep sigh that came from Aron before he gave her an answer.

"Rachel in all the time that we've known each other, you know you've never seen me with a woman. Not because I am hiding them, but because there was no woman that would interest me. But Becky...she is different. I tried keeping away from her. But that didn't last long. It didn't last even a day. Which makes me believe there could be something. But I won't rush things. I want to see where things go. I want to take it slow."

They continued to speak but I was not listening anymore.

His words kept repeating in my head.

Where things go.

They can't go anywhere, right?

We were complete opposites.

He was a successful businessman, and I was a failure in my field of work.

I was trying to get back on my feet and find myself after years of losing myself in the world of fashion.

We were just too different.

Right?

## Chapter 16 (Aron's POV)

When I came back to Becky's house in the evening, I wasn't expecting an interrogation.

But that's exactly what awaited me.

It was obvious Rachel was just worried about her best friend and it just made me like her more.

She really was perfect for Mason.

After she was done with interrogating me, we moved to more pleasant topics, and I enjoyed her company, but I was nervous as well.

I had no idea where these feelings had come from but all day, all I could think about was Becky.

This woman was driving me insane after only one glimpse at all the passion that was building between us.

But I was determined to see where things could go.

Maybe, just maybe, she could be the one to change my opinion about women.

After about 30 minutes she finally stepped into the living room.

And she took my breath away.

She was in a pair of simple jeans and a T-shirt that was a bit big on her, but she was still stunning.

And the fact her face was free of any make up was a huge turn on.

She managed to convince Rachel that Mason needed her, but I highly doubted it since Rachel's phone didn't ring while we were talking.

But I wasn't about to point it out because it meant I got to have Becky all to myself once Rachel left.

When she finally came back into the living room, she slumped next to me on the sofa with a heavy sigh and closed eyes.

And honestly, I thought I had better restraint on myself but who am I kidding.

I was on her like a starving man in seconds.

And if her moan was any indication, I'd say she didn't mind it at all.

My hands roamed all over her body, but it wasn't enough.

I was already hard, and I just wanted to continue where we left things yesterday.

So, I got rid of her clothes in record time, and she didn't fall behind. She removed my clothes just as fast as I did hers.

Now she was in front of me in only a pair of panties because she had no bra on under her T-shirt and a groan escaped me when I took in all her naked glory.

She was gorgeous.

I was trailing my gaze all over her body and I could sense she was doing the same with my body.

Suddenly her fingers started to push down my boxer briefs band, but I caught her hands.

"Now, now. I think I should get my turn first since I am your guest. What do you say?"

While speaking I already moved her panties to the side and slid a finger inside of her wet core.

So, the only response I got was a moan and I took it as her agreeing to my words.

I took one of her nipples into my mouth and her hands tangled into my hands, pulling me closer to her chest.

I devoured her like my favorite dessert.

My fingers kept pumping in and out of her wet core.

But it wasn't enough for me.

I started trailing kisses down her body, over her stomach and paused at her waist band.

She was begging for more in seconds, and I was a gentleman, so I gave her what she wanted.

I ripped those offending panties from her body and dive in right away.

She smelled and tasted like heaven.

And I didn't stop until I felt her legs shaking around my shoulders.

That's when I added a finger to the torture, and she exploded in my hands.

As she went over the edge a scream escaped her mouth with my name on her lips.

But I was far from over. We were just getting started.

I pulled down my boxer briefs and rolled a condom down my length in record time.

She didn't even manage to catch her breath from the orgasm that tore through her a few seconds ago, but I was already on her and positioned between her legs.

I was in her next thing you know, and a groan escaped me while she squeezed me with her walls.

"Damn you are so tight."

I didn't get any answer from her, nor did I wait for it.

I began moving.

It was a slow pace at first but once she scratched over my back with her nail all senses left me.

I started pounding into her like a rabid animal, but I didn't care.

It felt so fucking good.

And before I was ready, we were both nearing our climax.

It felt like it only lasted a few seconds and suddenly her walls squeezed me so tight I couldn't find my own release anymore.

My hands gave out and I was sprawled on top of her.

We were both trying to catch our breath.

After a few minutes I went to discard the condom.

When I came back, she was still lying on her back sprawled across the sofa and a chuckle escaped me.

"What are you chuckling at? My legs died! I can't move them. No, I don't even feel them!"

At her outrage and words, a laugh burster out of me.

"Honey, that just means I did my job right."

At that she started chuckling as well.

I stepped next to her and started to help her back in her clothes.

She looked at me in shock.

"Wha-what are you doing?"

"Helping you to get dressed. Then you will tell me what we are having for dinner, and I will warm it up."

She was still looking at me with shock in her eyes.

"Where did you come from?"

A laugh escaped me once more.

I managed to put her in a T-shirt and her pants and stood up.

I gave her a peck on the lips and pushed some hair behind her ear.

"It seems to me every last one of your exes was a piece of shit. But I am not like them. I know how to treat a woman."

Then I proceeded into the kitchen with her in my arms.

I put her down on one of the stools in the kitchen and went to the counter.

I found spaghetti Bolognese sitting there and I got down to heating it up.

"How'd you know it was my favorite?"

She burst out laughing.

"I didn't. It's one of Mason's favorite dishes. And mine as well."

"Looks like we have more in common than we thought."

We shared a smile, and I went back to work on our dinner.

## Chapter 17 (Becky's POV)

I was starting to believe that I was hallucinating, or I woke up in another universe.

Maybe I was still sleeping and today didn't even happen yet.

Because otherwise, I had no idea where Aron came from.

We all know about that logic. Before sex you help each other with clothes but after you are on your own.

But no, he helped me get dressed after we were done and carried me to the kitchen, where he was now heating our dinner.

So, excuse me if I was a bit shocked.

He prepared everything while I was still trying to get over the shock and maybe get my legs back into working.

Things like that just don't happen in real life.

But I guess I was being proved wrong at every turn we took tonight.

Dinner still smelled amazing and as soon as Aron sat down beside me, we dug in.

I'd say we worked up our appetite pretty well.

We ate our dinner in silence and Aron took both our empty plates into the sink.

"Don't you dare wash the dishes! I will do it later or tomorrow morning," I threatened him.

He turned my way with a soft smile playing on his lips.

"But that sounds unfair to me since you cooked."

I was ready to object when he stopped my words with his hand on my mouth.

"Nope. Heating dinner is not the same as cooking. So, I will do the dishes and you get that sexy ass of yours into the living room and find a good movie we can watch ok?"

His hand was still cowering my mouth so I could only nod my head at him.

"Good girl."

He removed his hand and at the same time, his lips found mine.

I have no idea what it was about this man, but I just couldn't get enough of him.

So, our kiss soon turned into a full-on steamy make-out session.

Which was completely ok in my book.

But it seems like Aron wouldn't forget about dirty dishes that easily.

"You really know how to tempt me, but I will do the dishes one way or another. If I have to make sure you can't feel your legs again before I do the dishes, I will do it willingly."

At his words, a whimper escaped me. I couldn't help it.

His words turned me on as no one else had before him.

A smirk crossed his lips.

Damn this man. He knew exactly what he was doing to me and my hormones.

"Be a good girl and do as I say."

This time he only pecked my lips, turned me around, and slapped me on the ass which made me gasp.

Not from the pain, but from the pleasure that shoots right to my core in seconds.

I hurried to the living room before I would embarrass myself even more with my horny traitorous hormones.

Ah, sue me.

You would feel the same if you had the kind of sex, I did an hour ago.

I was on the sofa going through the movie collection on my tv when my eyes began to feel heavy.

I was trying to stay awake, but I could feel it was a losing battle.

And before I knew it, I was out.

\*\*\*\*\*\*\*\*

I woke up feeling something heavy pressing against my stomach.

What the....?

I slowly opened my eyes and the first thing I realized was that I was in my bedroom.

And that heavy thing on my stomach was Aron's arm.

He stayed the night.

I was sure once he would find me sleeping, he would leave or at least sleep in the guest room or Mason's room like he did the previous night.

But no.

Instead of what I expected, he seemed to carry me to my bedroom and slept with me the whole night.

Even though we didn't do anything else but sleep.

I was not used to this kind of man.

Usually, if there wasn't sex involved, they simply took off.

But Aron proved to me with every passing second that he was different.

I tried to wiggle from under his arm without waking him up, but as soon as I moved, he tightened his grip around my waist.

"Where do you think you're going?"

His voice was husky from sleep, and it made my insides tighten at hearing it.

"Um, to make breakfast?"

It was meant to be a statement but instead, it came out as a question.

His eyes were still closed, and a soft chuckle escaped his lips.

"I already know what I want for breakfast."

"Just tell me and I'll make it for you. After all, you didn't have to carry me in my bedroom last night so I kind of owe you."

At that, his eyes popped open, and I was under him in just a few moments.

His eyes were practically glowing with anger and lust at the same time.

"Let's make one thing clear. You owe me nothing. You cooked us dinner and because I couldn't keep my hands off you, it got cold. We managed to take care of that and had an amazing dinner. I carried you to your bedroom because a woman like you deserves to sleep in a bed, not on the couch and I did it because I wanted, not because I had to."

I was so shocked by everything that I only managed to nod my head at him.

A smirk spread across his lips before he continued.

"Now about my breakfast. You see, it does not require any kind of cooking and you don't even have to move from bed."

I was confused at first.

What kind of breakfast could I have in my bedroom?

I never kept any food in this room.

The bedroom was meant for sleeping, not eating.

But then he started trailing kisses down my breasts and my stomach and to my surprise I realized I was still naked.

As I was busy processing everything, his lips found their target.

He sucked my clit into his mouth and suddenly it all became clear.

He wanted me for breakfast.

And he won't hear a single complaint about it from me.

As long as he kept delivering those fantastic orgasms I was totally on board.

And with Aron, it seemed I was only starting to get first glimpses at how a woman should -be treated.

One thing was for sure though.

Once he would be done with me, I would be ruined for any other man.

## Chapter 18 (Aron's POV)

After I and Becky had breakfast, this time it was food, we made our way together to the office.

I couldn't help but wonder what kind of assholes she dated in the past.

I was sitting in my office, just staring through the window when I realized I might be out of depth here with Becky.

I needed a woman's insight.

Calling my aunt about this kind of thing was out of the options.

Vicky as well. If I asked that woman about Becky so early in our relationship or whatever we had going on, I wouldn't hear the end of it, and she would scare Becky away for sure.

So, I only had one other choice, and it was overdue I gave her a call anyway.

She picked up the phone on the second ring, like always.

"Hello, there brother. How can I help you? I thought you forgot about me since you last called or texted me months ago."

I couldn't help but chuckle.

Ana was one of a kind.

Even though we were cousins, we grew up together and she always called me brother and I called her sister.

We were also as close as siblings and, in our book, we were just that. Siblings. Giving each other hell but having each other back at every turn.

"Hey, Ana. You know I could never forget about you. It's just been a really busy few months for me. You know how things are around here."

"Yeah, yeah. Don't get all grumpy on me right at the start of our conversation. What's up? Did mom tell you to call me and help me realize I don't need to become a lesbian?"

I burst out laughing. Damn, I almost forgot about that. Each time I tried to picture my aunt's face when Ana told her that I couldn't hold in the laugh that escaped me.

After a moment she started laughing as well and we both needed almost a full minute before we managed to get our breath back.

"Actually no, but we will get back to that. I know it's funny for us but one of these days your mother will have a heart attack because of you, young woman. First I wanted to ask you when you are coming home."

Suddenly there was a heavy kind of silence in the air between us and a sigh escaped her before she answered.

"I'm coming home next week, but I don't think I'll be going back to the university."

She was always so cheerful but right now she sounded as serious as ever and I could even hear a trace of defeat in her voice. Which was so unlike her.

We were both raised to never give up on our dreams, and she was pursuing her dream of becoming an artist, "Ana, talk to me. What happened?"

She chuckled at my words, but her chuckle was sad and empty.

"Nothing really. Don't worry about me, please. This is my decision and my life. And for once I will fix it on my own. Please. You've put your life on standby so many times because of me and I won't let you do it again. I promise it's nothing major."

It was hard for me to agree with her, but I could finally hear the determination in her voice. And I had a feeling she needed to do this on her own. For herself.

So, I reluctantly agreed, "Ok. But if you need anything you know where to find me."

The chuckle that escaped her this time was already more like her, "You know I do, but that's not the reason why you called me. Now spill it brother dearest. What bugs you?"

It was my turn to be on the hot chair it seems. I took a deep breath before I started speaking, "Ok. So, here's the short version. I met someone. She is perfect in any way possible and no I am not in love since I have known her for only a few days now, but you could say I like her a lot. But I have a problem. Seems to me that she was dating the worst assholes possible. Anything I do for her she thinks she owes me. And I can't help but feel like she thinks it's all just an act. Now if you could help me from a woman's point of view, what should I do to make her realize it's just who I am and not an act?"

"Hold on. You met someone and she is not all over you and your money? How is that even possible?"

The sarcasm in her words was really thick.

"Hardy-ha-ha. Not funny. Becky has her own money and doesn't need mine."

"Can I know her last name as well?"

"Collins. Why is that important now?"

Ana gasped so loudly at my words I had to move my phone a safe distance away from my ear, and good thing I did because the next thing I knew she was yelling at me, "Rebecca 'Becky' Collins? The Becky? The super-hot model Becky? Are you for real right now? You are banging probably the hottest person in London! Oh my God, how did you even meet her?"

"She is my assistant's best friend. And if you remember Mason? Well, she is his sister."

"Damn it. How did I not put those two together? Of course. And to answer your question. She probably was dating assholes all her life. That's the world of fashion you know. And men in those circles don't give a fuck about anyone else but themselves. So, the only thing you can do is be patient and show her how a real man treats his woman."

"But you know I am NOT a patient man Ana."

"Oh, believe me, Aron, I know. But if you want her as badly as I think you do, you will have to learn."

Fuck!

## Chapter 19 (Becky's POV)

I needed my best friend.

And I needed her as fast as possible.

But this day was going at a snail's pace, and I was starting to get nervous.

I needed Rachel and her advice.

I was out of my depths with Aron.

He was nothing like all my exes. He was kind and observant.

He paid attention to little things and that left me speechless.

I wanted to say that I was unaffected, but I wasn't.

Like I said before, I was out of my depths, so yes, I needed a good heart-to-heart with my best friend.

Suddenly Aron's door opened and the man in question came out of his office.

"Do you have any plans for this weekend?"

His question surprised me, which shouldn't really be a surprise anymore since he did this to me at every turn.

I tried to think if I had any plans but came up empty.

"Uhm, I guess I don't. Why?"

A beautiful smile spread across his handsome face, and I was only able to stare at him.

How is it not illegal to be this kind of handsome?

"Great. That makes it easier for me. I will pick you up on Saturday at 7 pm. Dress casually, but I do have something special in mind for us. And since you do have plans, well now you do I guess, it makes it easier because I don't have to tell you to cancel them."

With those words, he turned around and went back into his office and I was left staring at his closed door like an idiot with a wide-open mouth.

What in the ever-loving hell just happened?

I pulled my purse closer to me and started searching for my phone in a hurry.

Come on guys now it's EMERGENCY!

I dialed Rachel with shaking hands.

Thank God for once she wasn't busy with my brother.

"Hey, Becky. How is my best friend doing in her new job? Oh, and how was dinner yesterday? "

She was rambling like crazy and right now I didn't have time or patience for this.

"Rach! Please shut up for a second! I need your advice. And I need it badly."

She was quiet for a moment before I got any kind of response.

"Oh, can I speak already? Sorry. We will act like you didn't tell me to shut up, since you know how much I hate to hear those words and I know you are not such an evil bitch. Now for your problem. Sure shoot. What do you need?"

I chuckled at her words.

Sure, I knew she hated to hear someone telling her to shut up, but it was the only way to get her attention when she was rambling.

"I can't speak about it right now. Can I come over tonight?"

"You know you can. But why are we not meeting at your house? I know you don't like to come over if Mason is at home because you say your sugar levels rise above sky high."

"Aron is still staying with me."

My words were practically whispered because I was kind of afraid of her reaction and I also didn't want Aron to hear my conversation.

"Speak louder, woman I can't hear you!"

Of course, the only time I had to speak quietly was when my best friend decided to have bad hearing.

"Aron is still staying with me! Did you hear me this time?"

"Damn it! Don't yell at me!"

I sighed in frustration but reminded myself it was just her hormones.

"Like I said. I will come over around 5, OK?"

She agreed and we ended our call.

Now I only had to survive until 5 pm.

A piece of cake, right?

\*\*\*\*\*\*\*\*\*\*\*\*\*\*\*\*\*\*\*

Let me tell you something.

It wasn't a piece of cake. Not at all.

I had to hide each time Aron came out of his office or tried to look busy.

Today I couldn't deal with his behavior anymore.

He was just....too perfect for this world.

When the clock showed it was 4.25 it meant I only had 5 more minutes to endure, and my leg was nervously bouncing up and down.

At 4.30 I practically sprinted out of the building and hailed a cab that would take me to Rachel's house.

I was there a few minutes early, but I didn't care.

I marched right in after ringing the bell.

Since Rachel was expecting me, I knew the door would be unlocked.

I came into the living room only to find Rachel on the sofa watching a movie with a bowl of popcorn in her arms and she was bawling her eyes out.

Hormones.

I sat next to her and realized she was watching Titanic. Again. And like always she was crying.

It wasn't all hormones.

I picked up the remote and turned off the tv. I needed her help, and I needed it fast, "Hey! I was watching that!"

"And you can return to Jack and Rose once you help me out!"

At that moment Mason walked inside and when he saw us on the sofa, he started moving to the stairs to give us some privacy, but I stopped him, "Hold on. I might need your insight on some things as well since you are a man."

He stiffened for a moment but made his way to the living room.

When he sat down on the opposite sofa, I could see he was ready to kill someone, "Stop it, Mason. I need you not to lose your shit. And not to kill anyone."

"No promises sis. Spill what's going on!"

"Ok. Here goes nothing. Yesterday I slept with Aron. But the problem is he seems too good to be true. Now be honest with me. Is it an act or is he truly so different from anyone I ever dated?"

Mason watched me for a whole minute before he burst out laughing. I was speechless. I could just stare at my brother like he lost his ever-loving mind.

"Ah, sister dearest. No, it is not an act. I swear I tried to corrupt that man, but nothing works. I guess it's the way he was raised. But I will be the first to admit you found yourself a real problem. He is not like the guys you are used to dating. Once he sets his eyes on you, you are his and he won't stop at anything to get what he wants. I can't believe I didn't see this turn of events. You two are like a perfect match. But believe me. He is as stubborn as you are, if not even more."

Rachel kept nodding her head at Mason's words and I kept repeating those same words.

"So, you are trying to tell me, that I can trust him?" They both nodded their heads at my question, "I like him and that scares me shitless."

Rachel gave me a soft smile and grabbed my hand, giving it a light squeeze, "It's obvious you like him, or you wouldn't be here. But right now, I am wondering what you are still doing here. I think a nice man is waiting for you at home."

I jumped to my feet and ran to the door only to realize I forgot to give them both a proper hug goodbye. So, I turned around, hugged them, and ran to the door again, shouting goodbye as I went.

I could hear them chuckling, but I had no time. A handsome man was waiting for me. And I need to make him like me as much as I like him.

## Chapter 20 (Aron's POV)

I was sitting in the living room of Becky's house repeating a mantra that was supposed to calm down my frayed nerves.

It didn't help, damn it!

Be patient.

Be patient.

She will come home soon.

You can talk to her then.

Be patient.

I AM NOT A PATIENT MAN!

Sure, I can be patient when it comes to work. But even then, I am fighting with everything in me and am always a few steps ahead. That's why I always get what I want.

But with Becky, it was a different story.

All this was an unknown ground for me.

I wanted her. And my opinion was, I had to just get her out of my system.

She told me she is not one to pursue a relationship at this time.

That she is trying to find herself first after years of losing herself to the fashion world.

But even though I told myself every time that it was just a fleeting obsession, I couldn't ignore the voice at the back of my mind that kept questioning if it was really just that?

I was lost deep in my thoughts when suddenly the front door slammed open.

What the hell?

I was ready to check what was going on when a heavily intoxicated Becky stumbled into the living room.

"Well, hello there sexy boss man. I hope your night was as amazing as mine was."

She chuckled at the end of her statement, and I couldn't help it when my lips stretched into a gentle smile.

She was slurring so I guess she had a lot to drink since we drank pretty much the other night, and she wasn't as drunk as she was right now.

"My night was pretty laid back. But I did worry about you, young woman. Where were you?"

She tried glaring at me but with her wobbly stance it didn't end up being as scary as she intended. She looked...cute.

"You are neither my father nor my boyfriend. So, I don't have to tell you where I was. But since I want to tell you, I will. I was with my ex-agent. She has been trying to reach me since I fled from Paris. I did call her the day I landed and told her about my new job, but it was like she wanted to reach me even more after that. Weird woman this Margaret, I tell you. But she did try her best to shield me from things like the one that blew into my face the last time. So, I guess she is weird in a good way? Why is this room spinning?"

She was still rambling and trying to understand why her house was spinning. She really was drunk. And she was a funny drunk. I went to support her, and she put her weight onto me in no time, "You are so soft and hard at the same time."

I chuckled at her, but there was one thing in the back of my mind that was bothering me about her former agent. Somehow her name sounded familiar, but I had no idea where I had heard it before, "Tell me more about your former agent."

She lifted her head to look me in the eyes and I could see questions swimming in them even before she worded them, "Why? Do you want to sleep with her? If so let me tell you something mister. I don't give up on my man that easily. You gave me one night of pleasure and that is not enough in my book. That was just a start. Now you made me a starving woman and I want more."

I was trying to hold in my laughter as hard as I could, but it was not an easy task with her rambling, "Becky. You are the first woman in years to pique my interest and I am not done with you either. So, you don't have to worry about that."

At my words she gave me a smile that melted my frozen heart. She really was something else.

"Ok. In that case. Like I've told you. She is a weird person. I always had this weird feeling she cared more about my life back in London than about me as a person. I can't really explain it though. It was always just a feeling. But she did her job pretty well. Got me new gigs, sponsors etc. But now that I think about it, she always made sure I stayed in London if she could. When I accepted a gig in some other country she was always pissed and talking about not being able to look for someone if she is not in London. Don't know. Weird woman. But I wanted to travel the world. To see other places and enjoy the world of fashion as long as I could. And now that I am out of my business, she seems to be happy I lost my job and am no longer a model. She says it's because she knows how much I missed my family. But there is something else in those green eyes of hers. Oh, now that I think about it. Her eyes look almost like yours. But hers are greener where yours are a sexy mix of green and brown."

That weird feeling in the back of my mind kept reminding me those words should fire an alarm on my part somehow. But I had no idea why. Something sounded familiar in her words, but I couldn't pinpoint it.

"Ok young lady. Time to get you into bed, what do you say?"

"Ok. But just because I want to, not because you told me so. Will you stay the night with me?"

I agreed and got us both into her bed. I made us both ready for bed and cuddled next to her under the covers. Soon we both drifted into sleep land.

That night I dreamed about my biological mother. Her face was blurry, but her green eyes watched me with evil intentions. And all the while I could hear Becky's voice in the back of my mind, "Margaret...weird woman...green eyes...looks like your eyes..."

But as I woke up, I couldn't remember what my dream was about. Only those green eyes that kept haunting me throughout the night.

## Chapter 21 (Becky's POV)

It's been a pretty peaceful week.

Well apart from my drinking stunt on Monday.

Which is still a bit of a blur in my memories.

I can't remember most of the night.

I know I went out for a drink with Margaret, I ordered some whisky like always but that's it.

After my first glass my memory is blank.

Which is weird because I am not light weight.

There were days when I didn't eat at all and was drinking alcohol, but not once did my memory go blank.

And that kept bugging me throughout the week.

I also tried calling Margaret, but she didn't pick up or return any of my calls.

Something just didn't feel right about that Monday night.

But I had no time to dwell on it.

Aron will be home soon and then we are going out.

I still have no idea where he is taking me.

Me and Aron... We are great, you could say.

There is this side of him that he hides from the world.

A vulnerable side. But in the past few days I managed to get a few glimpses of that side as well.

Especially when he talks about his aunt or cousin.

They both sound like amazing ladies.

And underneath all that business look, Aron also hides a mischievous strike.

I couldn't help the chuckle that escaped me at remembering how he told me about Ana and her idea of becoming a lesbian.

I could practically see my mom's face if I told her something like this and it just made me laugh harder. I can just imagine what kind of trouble those two got into back in school.

He also told me his uncle died when Ana was only a few weeks old.

One night his aunt came home with Ana and found him stabbed in the back 6 times, lying in his own blood on the bathroom floor. They never found his killer. So up until today, more than 20 years later, his murder is still unsolved. His aunt never got married again or even dated anyone.

She says her husband was the love of her life and she would never disrespect him like that. It really was a beautiful thing to hear. Even an ice queen like me melted at that.

Right. Enough daydreaming.

I need to find clothes!

I started digging around my wardrobe.

Ok. He said something casual and not too fancy.

I decided on a neon green T-shirt that fit me like a glove and my favorite pair of jeans.

Of course, they made my ass look perfect duuh.

I paired it with my green all-stars, grabbed my jeans jacket and I was ready.

I was just coming downstairs when there was a knock at my door.

I went to open it and started laughing when I saw Aron standing there with a bouquet of roses in his hand.

"You know you live here at the moment, and you could come in right?"

His lips stretched into a soft smile, which in the past week I realized was reserved only for me, his aunt and cousin.

Everyone else got the fake smirk he always wore.

"Now what kind of date would that be if I just barged inside the house? I might be young, but I like to do things the old-fashioned way."

It took everything in me not to swoon at his words.

God help me, this man was perfect in every way possible.

And if I wasn't careful, I might fall for him.

I took a second to give him a once over.

He was wearing those jeans that fit him perfectly, a green button-down shirt, with a few buttons undone at the top.

His sleeves were rolled up and shoving me those muscular forearms.

Wait. What?

Since when did I develop a fetish for forearms?

Well guess it's more an Aron fetish than anything else.

I realized he asked me something and shook my head to get back to reality.

"I'm sorry. What?"

A chuckle escaped him before he repeated himself. "I asked if you are ready?"

"Oh yeah. Sure. Let's go."

He offered me his elbow and locked the door behind us.

He led me to his car, and we were on our way.

I couldn't help but feel nervous.

I have hated surprises since I was little, and that affection never changed.

"Can I know where we are going already?"

He just chuckled and shook his head no.

I was pouting and decided to turn my attention on the outside world.

Suddenly he took my hand in his and brought it up to his lips to give it a kiss.

"Did I tell you; you look beautiful? And we actually managed to match our outfits."

Qt his words I chuckled.

Damn him. I couldn't even be mad at him for long.

The car suddenly came to a stop, and I looked outside.

Our destination wasn't anything special to be honest.

We were in the nearby neighborhood that was known as the peaceful one.

There were houses with huge lawns in front, but it wasn't the pretentious type.

It was just enough to make you feel calm and at ease here.

I looked at Aron and I couldn't ignore the mischievous smile on his lips.

"Aron. What did you do?"

"Me? Nothing. I just brought you here for a nice dinner."

Something was fishy here.

"Ok. And who lives here?"

There was a spark in his eyes that told me whatever his plan was I wouldn't like it.

"Oh that. Just my aunt. And I guess Ana is already here as well since her car is in the driveway."

Yup. Not going to like it. I knew it.

Do you think I am allowed to have a panic attack right now? Or maybe a breakdown?

## Chapter 22 (Aron's POV)

I swear this whole situation would be hilarious if my "girlfriend" wouldn't look like she might just pass out.

"Girlfriend" because I have no idea how to describe what we have right now.

We spend some time together out of the office, well since we live together for the time being I'd say we spend almost every second together.

But we keep things professional in the office, while outside of it all bets are off.

And I would be lying if I told you I didn't enjoy every second of our time spent together.

But right now, she looked like she was on the verge of a panic attack.

Her eyes were as big as saucers, and she was shaking her head at me.

"No, no, no. Aron no. You can't do this to me. I've never done this. I will embarrass myself. No, no, no. I can't do this."

Now I realized I might make a mistake by bringing her here out of the blue, but right now we can't go back. We'll have to get through this together.

I made my way around the car, so I was standing in front of her now.

"Breath Becky. In, out. Come on. Do it with me."

She listened to my words and started to calm down slowly.

"There we go. Now don't panic, ok? It's not so bad. My aunt and cousin know about you, and they already love you. They can't wait to meet you. I am sure they already ambushed the window of the living room and are spying on us right now."

At my words, she managed to relax a bit more and even a soft chuckle escaped her. It brought a smile to my lips.

"Ok. I can do this. But promise me not to leave my side. I am not joking. I never did this before. I never met my boyfriend's parents."

Her words shocked me, and I am sure it was written all over my face, but it was something for another day.

I gave her a soft kiss before promising not to leave her side and we walked up the stairs to the front door, hand in hand.

As I predicted, the front door was pulled open before we even managed to ring the bell.

I shook my head while a smile was playing on my lips.

Aunt Lizz was standing at the door with a massive smile on her lips.

"My gosh. I already thought I wouldn't live long enough to see this day. But here you are. Sweetheart just from things Aron told me about you, you are a perfect match for him, and I am so glad to have you here in my home."

In seconds she pulled her from my hands and had her arms wrapped around her in a bear hug.

"Thank you, Mrs. McNamara. I am glad Aron brought me here tonight even if I had no clue until we arrived."

Damn. This woman threw me under the bus in seconds. But my smile remained on my lips.

I was also ready to receive my aunt's slap on the back of my head.

"I swear I raised you better than to lie to your woman!"

I chuckled at her.

"Yes, auntie you did. But she is a stubborn woman and if I told her the truth she wouldn't be standing here right now."

A stink eye was aimed my way from Becky, but I didn't care. I would make it up to her later.

"Well, honestly, he is probably right. It's my first time meeting my boyfriend's relatives and I would probably panic even worse than I did a moment ago in your driveway."

"Ah, my dear. Don't worry. Just forget about the fact it's a family dinner. Consider us friends, ok?"

She took Becky's hand, and I could only hear Becky agree with her.

But my mind was focused on the fact she called me her boyfriend.

Does it mean she accepted me officially?


**********

"So, you are trying to tell me, that this man right here that loves his rules and punctuality was once the opposite of that?"

If you thought my so-called girlfriend and both women, I loved most in my life were having a laugh at my dispense you guessed correctly.

Lizz was telling Becky stories about my not-so-perfect past.

And honestly, I didn't even mind it.

Because they were all having fun.

And what's better than seeing people you care about to be happy? If only it lasted for a few hours, it was more than enough in my book.

The dinner was over and a huge success. Like I told Becky, Aunt Lizz and Ana would love her and I was right.

Becky and Ana also already had plans for dinner in the future with Rachel.

Now we were just sitting in the living room, drinking coffee, and having fun.

Well, they were having fun, and I was desperately trying to turn the conversation in another direction.

Unsuccessfully as you can guess. Suddenly Becky's phone rang...

She took it out of her purse and from the look on her face I knew it was someone she had to answer, "Sorry, I just need to take this call fast."

We all just nodded our heads letting her know it was ok.

"Hey, Margareth. Yes, I am just at my boyfriend's family for dinner. Um yeah, sure just a second..."

She covered the speaker and turned my way to ask for the house address because Margaret needed to speak to her about something important.

I answered her and she relayed the information to her ex-manager, "I am so sorry for making my visit here so short, but I do have a few more minutes left before she arrives. She told me she'd call me once she arrives."

We continued talking like the call didn't even happen when suddenly there was a knock at the front door. I stood up and went to answer the door.

There stood a woman that looked somehow familiar to me, but I couldn't put a finger on it.

"Hey. You must be Margret. Becky is still inside with my aunt. You can come in if you'd like."

Her face was pure fakeness.

"Of course, dear. I'd love to come inside."

I moved away from the door to let her pass.

When we entered the living room though, the real chaos started.

"Maggy, what are you doing here?"

My aunt was the first to speak and I could see she knew the woman in our house.

Suddenly it all made sense to me, "You mean Maggy as your sister?"

I gritted out through my teeth. The woman in question turned around with her plastic smile firmly in place, "She means Maggy or Margaret as your mother."

Those words were the breaking point for my sanity.

I took a step closer to her and spoke slowly so she wouldn't miss one thing I told her, "The woman that raised me, and I consider my mother, is sitting right in front of you, and you are standing inside her living room. But you? You never were or ever will be my mother. The only thing you did for me was give birth to me. And then you abandoned me. So, excuse me, but your actions make you a little less than a stranger to me."

I could see a slight trace of hurt in her eyes, but I didn't care.

She hurt me far worse in the past, and I wanted nothing from this woman. With those words, I turned around and left my childhood home.

I just wanted to forget about the past few minutes of my life.

## Chapter 23 (Becky's POV)

Fuck, fuck, fuck!

I knew Margaret's interest in my personal life all of a sudden was weird, but I never expected such a huge portion of shit to hit the fan!

I was still trying to get my head around the fact that she was Aron's mother.

And knowing him as I know him now, I was afraid to think what it meant for us and our fresh relationship.

And how could I even blame him? Knowing his story from the start, especially the beginning that concerns the woman that was standing in front of me right this second, while the man I cared about stormed outside.

He probably thought I betrayed him and did all this on purpose.

Sisters were still throwing daggers at each other while I was speechless.

I could see that Ana knew nothing about the woman standing in front of us.

Which confirmed the story Aron told me a few days ago.

She never cared enough to even show her face in this town. Until the day I told her about my new boss and his name.

I shook myself out of my trance and decided to end this painful silence.

I took a slow step forward, so I was now standing in front of Margareth.

"I knew you were a heartless bitch, but all this time I thought it was the world of fashion that made you the way you are today, but no. You were like this even before you put a foot inside my world. But right now, there are no words that could describe how grateful I am that I don't have to work with you, not even a minute of my precious time. And believe me when I tell you, I will ruin you. I will hit where it hurts the most, which in your case is money."

She was staring at me with her mouth gaping and trying to come up with something to say but all she managed was to keep opening and closing her mouth.

I was ready to walk away and see if Aron was still standing in the driveway, hoping he was waiting for me.

But suddenly I remembered something.

"Oh, I almost forgot what I promised to my boyfriend."

"What...?"

Her words were cut off by a loud slap that hit her across her face.

I could hear Lizz gasp behind me and Ana laughing, but I was done. My priority was to find Aron and tell him I had no idea who she was, to make things right.

I was putting my shoes on in a hurry when suddenly a pair of arms wrapped around me.

When I turned around Ana stood there with a shit-eating grin on her face, but when I went to ask her what that was all about, she beat me to it.

"You and I, Becky are going to be really good friends. For the first time since I decided to quit studying, I am happy about my decision and looking forward to something, that being hanging around with you."

She wrapped me in another one of her bear hugs and whispered in my ears.

"You have no idea how much it means to me what you did for Aron there. He might not be my brother by blood, but I always saw him as my brother. And knowing he is not alone right now with the pain of today's day; I can't describe how grateful I really am to you really."

A soft smile crossed my face, and I returned her embrace.

"No worries, Ana. Someone had to put her in her place. And I would love to be friends with you like I've told you at dinner already. You have my number so just give me a call once you move back completely and I and Rach can meet you for some drinks."

We said our goodbye and I practically ran out of the house only to bump into something hard. Well, actually it was someone.

Thank God he was strong and ready to catch me, or I'd have a bruised ss right now.

But I had no time to think about anything, I had to make sure he knew the truth.

"Aron, I had no idea who she was, I swear, or I would never ever stay in contact with her, or even less bring her here. I know what she did to you, and there is no way in hell I would do anything like this to you. Please you have to believe me..." suddenly my rambling was cut off by a pair of soft lips.

The kiss got heated in seconds and his hands were wandering all over my body, where they could reach. If you ask me, I'd say he was trying to put all his frustration into this kiss.

And honestly, I had no objections. I gave as hard as he did. The kiss continued until we were both breathless.

We pulled apart both gasping for air, and his hand was still resting on my ass, patting it softly a few seconds passed before he spoke his first words since I came out of the house and almost ran him over, "I believe you. Now move your sexy ass in my car. We are going somewhere."

I was speechless and couldn't even find my voice if my life depended on it.

So, I did the only thing any sane person would do in such a situation.

I quickly kissed him one more time and climbed into his car, because I had a feeling, he had more of those kisses in store for me, and who would ever say no to something like this?

He threw a devilish smirk paired with a wink my way and climbed behind the wheel. And off we go.

Destination: unknown.

Anticipation: sky high.

Adventure, and steamy moments, here we come.

Well, fingers crossed that my theory turns out to be what I wanted it to be.

## Chapter 24 (Aron's POV)

I was going at least 50 over the speed limit but it was still not fast enough for my taste.

I needed Becky. I needed her right now.

The rage inside me was something out of this world.

All I could think about was that woman and her audacity to even utter the words mother.

She was never my mother.

Not in any other meaning than she gave birth to me.

And in my book that is not a true mother.

My aunt raised me and gave me support when I needed it the most.

She helped me build my business from the ground up.

So, she was the real mother to me.

And I could never repay her for everything she did for me.

But right now, all I could think about as an escape route was being buried deep in Becky.

I wanted to feel her in my arms, feel her walls squeeze my cock.

To lose myself in her and forget about everything and everyone except her.

But I had to get her to the destination I had in mind first.

I was going to a hill that I knew was not popular.

I knew that because every time I wanted to clear my head and be alone for some time, I drove there.

And in all the years I went there, not once did I meet anyone up there.

So, we were going there, but today of all days the drive seemed to be extra-long.

Finally, I saw the clearing in front of us.

My car came to a screeching halt from the force I used to stop it.

In seconds I had Becky's seatbelt off, and I pulled her right into my arms.

All she managed to utter was a small screech before my lips were on hers and I successfully silenced her in seconds with a passionate kiss.

A moan escaped her when my hands found her waist and their way under her shirt.

There was no time to get her naked and after all, we were in a car, and even though I never met anyone here I wasn't willing to take any chances when it came to Becky.

Her naked body was only for my eyes to see.

We were both breathless in seconds, so I had to move away from her lips for a moment or two, but I wasn't about to leave her skin, so I continued kissing her down her throat and left some love bites on the way.

The whole world should know she belongs to me and me alone.

In a normal state, those thoughts would give me a small panic attack, but I was in a weird state right now and I didn't care at all. At this moment she was mine and somehow, I felt this feeling wouldn't change any time soon.

When did I become so possessive you wonder?

I have no fucking clue! But as I already said, I fucking don't care!

She felt too good in my arms to doubt anything.

Sweet moans escaped her mouth while my hands travelled over her upper body and my lips devoured her throat and ear lobes.

But it wasn't enough, so I made fast work of her button and zipper on her jeans.

"Get them off for me, beautiful."

I managed to mumble those words between kisses that were raining on her skin.

"I can do that, but you make fast work off your pants in the meantime."

Her voice was as breathless as mine was, and I obeyed her order right away.

After all, we had the same outcome in mind.

In seconds we made room for what we had in mind, and she was on my lap again.

Without any warning, she slid down my length and all I could do was groan with satisfaction.

She started moving before I was even ready.

The feeling was overwhelming and not enough at the same time.

I grabbed her hips and started pushing her on my length with more force.

As I did it a scream escaped her and for a second, I froze, thinking I had hurt her.

"Don't you dare stop! Move! I want more of that!"

Looks like my lady was a bossy one, and who was I to obey direct orders?

I started guiding her up and down my length with more force thus time.

Each time I was balls deep inside her a scream escaped her.

We have just begun our forbidden action, but I could already feel her squeezing my dick with her inner walls.

But I had to make this last.

One hand left her hip, so I could move it between our joined bodies and push her clit, so she would fall over the edge.

And she did just that, with my name on her lips.

I had to hold back with an extra effort to not blow my load too fast.

I wanted more. Much, much more.

As her aftershocks subsided, I started moving inside her again.

Once more I started to ram into her hard and she loved every second of it judging by the hold she had on my shoulders.

I could feel myself getting close again and this time there was no way I could hold back.

So, I put my finger on her clit once more and took her earlobe between my teeth.

"Come for me. One more time."

She was panting and squeezing my shoulders as if her life depended on it.

I could also feel she was close already because her pussy started clamping down on my dick.

But I needed her to come with me.

So, I did the only thing any sane man would do in my position.

I bit on her earlobe while my finger pushed a bit harder on her clit and all the time, I didn't slow down my pumping.

Before I knew it, she came with a scream and my name on her lips once again and I followed her a moment later.

She fell limp across my upper body, and I wrapped my arms tightly around her waist.

"Thank you for cooperating and helping me. I needed this."

At my words, she lifted her head.

There was a beautiful blush on her cheeks and a smile on her lips.

"Whenever you need this kind of stress relief, I am the right person for you."

For a moment we were both silent but then we burst out laughing.

In the back of my mind, I could hear my subconscious warning me to be careful or Becky might become my person in many ways and aspects.

But the real question was, would that be so bad?

## Chapter 25 (Becky's POV)

"Ewww! Shut up Becky! I don't want to hear any details about my brothers' sex life!"

Ana's face was scrunched up in disgust while me and Rachel were crying fat tears of laughter.

Let me fill you in on the past 3 months a little.

Me and Aron are still together and honestly, it's been the best 3 months of my life.

After a month of our relationship, we came out and surprisingly everyone in the company was really accepting of the fact that we shared the same bed.

Aron also never managed to move back to his house, at the moment we are thinking about selling it since we like our living arrangements as they are.

In this time Ana also became a part of our friendship circle that got upgraded from duo to trio.

Lizz is also the best, supporting us, calling us over for dinner at least a few times each month.

You probably wonder what happened with Margareth.

Honestly? I have no idea and I can't say I care.

I had no desire to have such a bitter and money hungry person in my life or Aron's for that matter.

But right now, it was our usual Thursday girl night. Aron and Mason were back at my house, well mine and Aron's and we girls were hanging at Rachel's. And as you probably guessed, we were discussing our love lives. But we had a problem. My brother is my best friend's boyfriend, and my boyfriend is my other best friend's brother.

So, at each story one of us, one was cowering her ears so as not to hear the details. Well except for Ana. And when we are at that part already... "Hey Ana, what about you? Any boys?"

Suddenly her face fell, and she was serious in moments, "Not really. There was one, but it just would never work out."

That statement perked up my interest badly.

"Details woman! And no, you can not back off. We are best friends, remember?"

Reluctance was written all over her face, but I could see it clearly the moment she decided to share.

"Ok. But promise me you won't say a word to Aron or Mason please?"

She waited for us to nod our heads before she took a deep breath and continued speaking.

"So...He comes from a really wealthy family. And it was all great between us. We met in our first year at college and just clicked right away you know. We started as friends, but one night we went out together and he admitted he liked me as more than just a friend and honestly the feelings were mutual. So, we started dating. And like I said, it was all perfect. Until one day his soon to be wife showed up at campus. He didn't even tell me himself. I had to hear it from her. Together with a big collection of nasty words. They had an arranged marriage planned. And the date is already set, and people invited etc. So there really isn't much I can do to change things. And as you can guess I packed my things and left campus and college after one week of hiding from the man I love."

At the end of her speech there were tears running down her face and my heart ached for her.

So young, but already heartbroken. Life really wasn't fair. Sure, she was a few years older than me and Rachel, but she still wasn't even 35 years old. So, in my book that was still too young for a broken heart.

Also let's get one thing straight. She was in college at this age only because she accepted Aron's help with the costs only a few years ago. So now she was taking classes for adults in a separate department from regular students.

Well not anymore it seemed.

"So, you just walked away? Did you ask him for his side of the story?"

She gave me a sad smile, while tears were still running down her face and her eyes were already filled with new ones, "Why? In all the time we knew each other not once did he mention her. Also, she showed me their wedding invitation. So, there is no doubt about her story. Why else would she have the invitation?"

I couldn't argue her logic even if I wanted too desperately.

Suddenly Rachel jumped from her position between me and Ana, "We need ice cream. And you both need more wine!"

Before we could even object she ran to the kitchen. We exchanged glances and burst out laughing, "She just wants more ice cream and uses your story as an excuse, so she won't feel so bad about it."

"I know! But I won't argue with a pregnant woman! I might be clueless but even I know it wouldn't end well for me!"

We were still giggling like two schoolgirls, but there really wasn't much we could do about it.

Rachel was obsessed with ice cream in the past month and used us as an excuse each time we had our night. We tried to tell her we are not judging her, but she wouldn't hear it, saying she was getting fat and that it helped if she shared the ice cream.

But we never got any ice cream.

"Ok. So, let's just pretend we don't notice and split the wine while she eats her ice cream. Again."

We just burst out laughing once more when Rachel came back into the living room.

"What's so funny?"

"Nothing Rach. We were just trying to picture Aron and Mason with pink bow ties that you chose for them for your wedding."

And now that I thought about it, I burst out laughing because of that picture for real, "Hey, it's not so bad!" Rachel tried to defend her taste.

"No, it's even worse!"

And at that, all three of us started laughing like crazy.

Damn it was good to have my girls by my side.

## Chapter 26 (Aron's POV)

It was another rainy day in London.

No surprise there, right?

I have no idea how people got used to it.

A few days a month would be ok. But in our case, we had sun a few days a month but other days it was rain, rain, and guess what? More freaking rain!

But never mind my ranting.

If I don't count the rainy weather, I was in a pretty good mood.

I woke up today to a beauty between my legs.

At first, I thought I was dreaming, but the closer I got to my release, the more obvious it became that she actually had my dick in her mouth as a way to wake me up.

Of course, I returned the favour. Twice.

Now I was sitting in my office, and unlucky me, today both my assistants left me.

They were on some wedding assignment or what the hell I know what it was.

I am just a man after all.

So, I decided to leave my office phone detached today.

Well, I actually unplugged it from electricity.

What? If I answered the phone every two seconds, I wouldn't manage to get any work done.

So, whoever needed something for me either had my phone or wasn't important at this moment.

I swear Rachel and Becky must've been some kind of robots to handle it all without a breakdown.

Or maybe it was just because we all know women are better at multitasking.

Yeah. Must be that.

So, as I said.

I was sitting in my office, getting some work done when suddenly there was a knock at my door. Because the door was closed, I told the person standing in front of it to come in.

But when the person entered, and I lifted my head I regretted it right away.

"What are you doing here? You are neither welcome here nor in my life! I will give you exactly a minute to turn around and leave my office!"

At my words I expected some fear, or an expression filled with hurt and regret, but instead she gave me an evil smirk.

Oh yes of course. If you didn't guess it already, my biological mother came by my office.

Unfortunately.

"Now Aron. Is that any way to greet your mother?"

I could almost laugh at her words.

But since I was raised better, I decided to hold it in.

"Right. What do you want?"

Her smirk slipped at my words, but an evil glint remained in her eyes.

"You see, I kind of made a name for myself years ago. And I managed to do that thanks to your stupid girlfriend."

My fists were clenched under the table, and I was grinding my teeth really hard from all the anger I felt at her words. But I managed to not interrupt her. The sooner she told me what she had on her mind, the sooner she would leave me alone.

"So, when she got tangled with that idiot Gareth, she pulled me under as well. Now, since you and I have a past, she won't pick up my calls and she is determined not to return to the world of fashion. But you see, I can't get back to where I was without her. Well honestly even with her it would be hard because she did a huge amount of damage to her picture."

When she finished her little speech, she looked at me expectantly.

"That's it? I have no idea what I have to do with any of this?"

Her smirk was back firmly in its place.

"I am glad you asked. So far you have nothing to do with it. But you come into the picture now."

Her words somehow didn't sit well with me. Not at all. I knew she was an evil woman but somehow, I had a feeling what she had to tell me would be on another level even for a woman like her. And unfortunately, I was right.

"You see, I need Becky to return to the fashion world. And right now, she has you and is not willing to leave. So, what you will do for your beloved mother is break her heart. And once you do that, she will have no reason to stay here anymore. That way you can be free of me again and I get my lifestyle back."

I couldn't help it when I burst out laughing at her crazy idea.

She actually thought I would go with her plan.

"You are even crazier than I thought if you believed I would leave Becky. Especially for you."

I said those words with determination.

But her smirk only grew at my words.

"But you see, I know you will. Because you love her. And if you decide to not turn my plan into a reality, I am afraid I will be forced to ruin the rest of Becky's reputation. I was with her since she started her career after all. So, I know all her dirty little secrets. But that's not my main weapon. Becky forgot I have her passwords, so I have access to all her ways of communication."

Oh shit!

I could feel all my blood draining from my face and cold sweat running down my back, because I had a suspicion where this was going. And if I was right, we were fucked.

And my fears were confirmed with Margreth's next words.

"I have all her naked pictures she sent you a few days ago. So, believe me. If I don't get what I want, those pictures will end up being the cover of every tabloid in the United Kingdom, if not in the whole world. And don't even think about telling her. Your beloved auntie will lose her house if you do."

My shoulders slumped because I realized there was no way out.

I had to break the heart of the only woman I ever loved.

And I didn't even have a chance to tell her.

Now it looks like I never will.

## Chapter 27 (Becky's POV)

If you asked me about regrets right now, I'd tell you I had none.

Life is great at the moment.

I finished all the wedding shopping with Rachel, and she just dropped me in front of my house.

So, I was just looking forward to a nice evening of relaxing with the man I love.

Yes, you read it correctly. I love him. But I still didn't tell him.

Honestly, he will be the first man to hear those words from me., besides Mason, but he is my brother so that doesn't count.

I decided to tell him today because those words threatened to spill out of my mouth on their own.

But I was scared shitless. I had no idea how Aron would react.

Sure, we had the best time together and even when we argued we made it better afterwards. In the bedroom of course.

Well, I guess there's no better time than right now.

So, I entered my house with a huge grin on my face and nervous butterflies in my stomach. "Aron! I'm home."

The first thing that made me pause in my tracks was the fact that I didn't get any response.

But maybe he just didn't hear me, right? Let's not make a huge deal out of it. Breathe in, breathe out. I exchanged my shoes for a pair of slippers and entered the living room.

To my surprise Aron was sitting there with his head in his hands. I don't like this, "Aron? Baby? Didn't you hear me when I came in? Is something wrong?"

I could see my voice startled him. It was like he was lost in his thoughts.

But when he lifted his head, I could clearly see pain and sadness written all over his handsome face.

And that's when panic hit me.

"Is Lizz, ok? Is it Ana? Speak to me, damn it! What's wrong?!"

He gave me a soft smile at my words, but it didn't reach his eyes and it wasn't even one bit happy.

"Come here Becks. We need to talk."

Those words. THE WORDS!

It made me freeze on the spot.

No, no, no! Not now! Not when I finally found someone I actually love! Damn you universe!

Thank God I managed to find my voice at that moment, "I'd rather stand, thank you."

His eyes once more looked at the floor and a heavy sigh escaped his lips.

The silence between us stretched on and on and I was starting to become even more nervous.

But he finally spoke. Even though it would be better if he stayed quiet.

Because his next words ripped my heart right out of my chest.

"This isn't working Becky. You and me. Us. It's not enough for me. Sure, we have fun together, but I don't see you in my future. And I don't want to lead you on. So, I think it's best if we break up."

Those words, spoken with such calmness, ruined me.

But surprisingly I managed not to fall on my knees and burst into tears.

Yes, it hurt like hell, but I wouldn't give him the satisfaction of seeing me break down.

No. That would happen later.

Once I'm alone with my ice cream.

"Get out."

Wait.

Did I really just say that?

Yes, I did!

And I meant every word of it.

But it was obvious those were not the words he expected to hear from me, and honestly neither did I. But it was what I needed right now. I needed to be alone, so I could cry my heart out.

You want to know the worst part?

Well, that would be the next thing he did.

He was just watching me for a few moments and then he stood and nodded his head and started walking towards the front door.

But I forgot I was still standing in the doorway of the living room and if he wanted to reach the front door, he had to pass me.

And when he did, he stopped next to me and kissed my cheek with words that kept ringing in my ears even long after he was gone.

"I wish things would be different. But I promise, one day you will understand the reasons behind my actions."

I could swear his voice shook at the end like he was battling his own tears from falling, but I didn't dare turn around and check, or I'd end up being the one in tears.

After those words, he simply left.

And I just stood there, looking at the place where he was sitting just moments ago.

My legs started to shake, and I slid down the doorway and sat my but on the floor.

How could I be so stupid?

I fell in love for the first time in my life, but I fell for a man that didn't even like me anymore.

I didn't even realize when I started crying and neither did, I have any idea how long I was sitting there.

Suddenly my doorbell rang, but I just wanted to be alone and to be honest I had no strength to even stand up from my position on the floor.

But I guess I didn't have to worry about that, because my best friends just opened the front doors and barged into my home.

"I swear, he will die. I don't care if we are related, he is a dead man."

I lifted my head to see Ana and Rachel standing in front of me with frowns on their faces and anger written in their eyes.

When I saw them, the dam broke completely and I started crying for real, with huge tears, sobbing, hiccupping…you get the picture.

It really was a pitiful sight.

But everyone deserves to have a breakdown once in a while.

Girls helped me to get up from the floor and move my ass to the couch.

In seconds there were so many sweets on my table that I felt fat just by looking at it.

But there was also wine and whiskey.

You can guess only once which one I chose.

But I had to ask Rachel and Ana one thing though.

"I'm kind of glad to see you guys here, but how did you know I needed you?"

At my words they both hugged me, each from one side.

"Aron called me, and I called Rachel. He pretty much admitted what a bastard he is and sealed the future of his peanuts. Now we won't waste any more time on that asshole I call my brother, instead we will drink, eat, watch movies and forget about reality for one night."

And so, drinking away the pain and sadness began.

Hopefully tomorrow morning, my head will hurt so much, I would forget about the pain in my heart.

Either way, I had my girls, and that was the most important thing right now.

Chapter 28 (Aron's POV)

I was counting down the minutes until my death arrived in the form of my best friend Mason.

Ok I might be a bit too dramatic.

Or maybe not.

He never was against me and Becky dating, but he warned me not to break her heart or he would break my neck.

So, as I did what I promised not to do, now I was waiting patiently to accept the consequences.

I was surprised though.

Because almost 6 hours passed already and it was close to midnight now, but there was no sign of Mason.

But just as that thought crossed my mind a key could be heard turning in the lock of my front door.

Before he could start shouting, I spoke, to tell him I'm in the living room.

And when he came around the corner there was rage written all over his face.

But still he wasn't half as pissed as I expected him to be.

"What gives?"

I was looking at him with wide eyes and probably looked like an idiot.

"Don't worry. I am pissed. You have no idea how much. But if I hurt you, Becky won't ever forgive me. Also, I had some time to think before I came here. And I came to a conclusion. I just need you to confirm it for me. Deal?"

I was dumbfounded so all I managed was a nod.

"Ok. So, I was just going through our security footage from the company. And to my surprise I saw a woman enter your office and quite a while later exit it with an evil grin on her face. Now first she looked at least 20 years older than you and I hope your taste didn't get so fucked up, also a woman after sex is unable to wear an evil smile on her face. But what hit me as the weirdest thing was when you came out of your office a few moments later with the saddest face I've ever seen. And a few hours later my fiancé sends me a text that says I need to castrate my best friend because he hurt my sister. Now spill it. Who was that woman and what did she want?"

Shit.

I should know this wouldn't go unnoticed on Mason's side.

He checked our cameras on a daily basis so it shouldn't surprise me honestly.

I was thinking about lying to him for a moment but when I looked at his face and saw determination written in his eyes, I knew I better tell him the truth.

"Ok. Now first I want you to know I love your sister more than I ever loved anyone. Breaking her heart was the hardest thing I ever did, because in the process I broke my own heart as well. And second, that was my biological mother. Turns out she was Becky's manager since she started her career in the world of fashion. And Becky refused to return to that world or to work with Margareth again once she realized who she was. But Margareth wants her money and lifestyle back and she can't have that without Becky. So, she came to my office to black mail me. A few days ago, Becky sent me some...uhm...adult pictures. And Margreth still has access to all her texts, phone calls history, social media accounts etc. And so, she found those pictures. And she threatened to send them to tabloids across the world and ruin Becky completely if I don't break up with her."

I stopped there for a moment so Mason could process everything.

He looked lost in his thoughts for a while before he spoke.

"Ok. A few things now make sense. But why would she want you to break up with the woman you love? I get it. She is a bitch, but I thought every mother wanted her kids to be happy."

A chuckle escaped me, but it lacked humor because nothing was really funny at that moment. It was just absurd to the point you had to laugh.

"Well, every mother except mine you see. Her theory is if we broke up, Becky wouldn't have anyone holding her back anymore and she would return to the world of fashion and back into her greedy claws."

In seconds Mason understood my point and my reasons for breaking up with Becky.

"That bitch! But I do have some bad news for her. Becky decided to quit almost a year ago already. She was just waiting to finish the project they were working on at the moment. She told me she misses our parents and Rachel and even me. And she couldn't do it anymore. She also always wanted a family and with her line of work that would be impossible."

I could feel a stone being lifted from my chest at his words.

At least she would stay in London. And find someone with a normal family, not a crazy mother like mine was.

"Stop that train of thoughts right away Aron. We are getting you and Becky back together or I won't marry Rachel. And we both know the chances of that happening are even lower than zero."

I looked at him with doubt, but I had no time to ask him what he had in mind.

"First we need to delete those photos from everywhere and I will need a huge amount of peroxide afterwards to clean my eyes. Then we get down to planning how to convince Becky to give you another chance. I might have an idea, but it needs some work."

There was no way in hell I would turn down help to get back the woman of my dreams.

"I am in. Tell me what to do."

Get ready Becky.

I will show you just how badly I love you.

And this time I am not letting her go.

Even though I lost her only a few hours ago, those hours were the most miserable hours of my life.

So, it's time to get my woman back where she belongs.

Next to me.

## Chapter 29 (Becky's POV)

I was a miserable woman for more than a week already.

And even now, Aron didn't stop sending me texts every day.

Like what the hell dude? He broke up with me but wasn't willing to let me get over him.

So right now, I was blasting music on my earphones so loud I could turn off everything else.

I was also cleaning my house.

After all, I had to finally get rid of all the evidence of Aron ever living here.

I didn't want to be reminded of him every day after all.

I also had to get my phone number changed as soon as possible, but I just didn't really feel like going out of my house just yet.

Maybe in a couple of days. But definitely not today.

So, I continued cleaning and singing to the songs playing in my head.

Of course, it was a special playlist made for a broken heart.

So, there were songs such as, Didn't I? You broke me first, leave before I love you, and so on.

I guess you get what I mean.

Suddenly my singing got cut off by a ping from my phone alerting me that I had a message waiting for me.

I huffed in exasperation but still took out my phone to check who was disturbing my pity party.

To my surprise- not really- it was Rachel and Ana in our group chat.

Ana: Hey girls. Are we still up for tonight?

Damn it. I forgot. They wanted to take me out and cheer me up.

But I was really, really not in the mood.

I was thinking about a good excuse when another text came through.

Rachel: Yep. We are still on, and Becky if you are not lying dead in some hole, no excuse will get you out of our night.

Damn it!

Sometimes it was not good to have a best friend that knew you practically since you were born.

Ah, I give up. Sometimes it is best to admit defeat.

Becky: Fine. Pick me up at 6.

They both gave me a thumbs-up and heart emoji and that was it.

I still had 2 hours to get ready but if I wanted to look presentable, I had to hurry.

15 minutes before the girls were going to arrive, I was all done.

I had a light blue dress that hugged my upper body perfectly but flared out from the waist down.

I curled my hair and pinned it back from my face, adding some light makeup and earrings that my parents gave me on my 18th birthday.

Just when I was done making sure it was all as I wanted it to be, girls arrived and blasted the horn to let me know.

I grabbed my purse, locked the door behind me, and joined them.

Tonight, we were expanding our circle once more and adding another person. Vicky.

So right now, we were on our way to her restaurant and honestly, I was kind of excited.

Once we parked the car, we entered Vicky's place and as soon as we did, she jumped on us, starting us in the process.

"You girls have no idea how happy you made me by inviting me tonight."

All three of us chuckled at her enthusiasm, but I did remember Aron telling me that most women found her intimidating and stayed clear of her.

Which I kind of found funny.

Sure, she was over the top happy all the time, but she was also the sweetest person I ever knew, and I think I knew quite a few people.

When we finished our hug, she took us to a table for four and told us to take a seat while she checked on the food and brought our drinks.

So far, I haven't regretted my decision to go out tonight.

The evening was nice and maybe the company of my friends was exactly what I needed for my broken heart.

A few minutes later a delivery boy stopped at our table, and I looked at him confused when he said my name.

"Uhm yes, that would be me. Why?"

A huge grin spread across his face at my words.

"Thank God. This place is so crowded that I feared it would take me hours to find you. Here I have a card for you."

As I took the card, I turned it over in my hand to see who it was from but no name other than mine was written on it and underneath was a message.

*We first met here for lunch,*

*I felt you were special, call it a hunch.*

*Next time it was just a drink,*

*But the evening was over in a blink.*

*Maybe I messed things up,*

*But remember this tonight,*

*You are always on my mind.*

*Xoxo*

I was looking at the card in my hand with confusion written all over my face.

What the hell?

When I lifted my head all three of my friends were looking at me expectantly.

But since I had no idea what this was supposed to mean I just shrugged my shoulders and started chatting with them again.

They wanted to know about the card but as I was not willing to tell them anything they dropped it.

Our food had just arrived and was placed in front of us when I noticed the second card, pinned under my plate.

I lifted it slowly and again there was no name except mine on it, so I started reading it.


*You made your way into my heart with such speed,*

*I had no time to go over the fine print.*

*But suddenly it all felt perfect in my life,*

*And someone decided to mess it up.*

*I said the final words of course,*

*But try to ask yourself,*

*Did it sound like the words that came from the soul?*

*Or like someone tried to ruin it all?*

*There will be another card coming your way.*

*I will reveal myself after that,*

*But be prepared because this time, I am going to stay.*

*Xoxo*

I had a feeling who was sending me these cards, but I didn't quite understand his words.

Hopefully, the last card will make things clear to me.

The girls wanted to know about those mystery cards and this time I told them. Even who I was thinking was behind it.

Ana confirmed my suspicions and Rachel and Vicky just nodded their heads letting me know they agreed. So, we confirmed it. Aron was my mystery man.  But what was his point? Well, guess I had to wait and see when the third card arrived.

And I didn't have to wait for long. A few minutes later it arrived with my dessert. But there was still no Aron in sight, so I got to reading it.  This time though it wasn't a poem.


*Dear Becky.*

*I know I messed things up big time.*

*But know that when I broke your heart, I broke mine as well.*

*Leaving you was the hardest thing I ever did, but I had to do it.*

*I had to protect you from the evil person in my life.*

*I wish I could say this story is taken care of, but she would probably continue to mess with our relationship.*

*That is if you are willing to give me another chance.*

*Always yours Aron*

*Xoxo*

My eyes started to tear up when I lifted my head only to realize I was now sitting with Aron and my friends were nowhere to be seen.

Traitors.

"Hey, Becks. I know it's no excuse for what I did to you, but I swear I had a good reason. My mother wanted to ruin your reputation and I couldn't let her do that. But when I told everything to Mason, I realized I don't have to fear her. We took care of her threats and are building up a case against her, to get her away from us both. Now the only question I have is if you are willing to forgive me and give me another chance?"

I only thought about it for a minute before planting my lips on his and letting him know my answer.

But if he thought he was getting off the hook that easily, he was wrong.

As I moved away from him, I gave him a stern look before speaking.

"You ever pull that kind of stunt again, and I will castrate you on the spot. Are we clear?"

He laughed and gave me a light peck before he answered.

"Understood. And if you were wondering, I love you, Becky."

Am I weird to melt at those words? I think not.

"I love you as well Aron."

You can guess that night wasn't long enough for all the make-up sex we had planned.

## Epilogue (Aron's POV)

A few months later

Candles, check.

Roses, check.

Wine, check.

Music, check.

I think I have it all set for our 6 months anniversary.

At least I hope so.

Let me bring you up to speed.

Rachel and Mason got married a month ago.

I was Mason's best man and Becky was Rahel's maid of honour.

Then a week ago, Rachel gave birth to a beautiful little angel.

They named her Rebecka after the most brilliant and beautiful woman, my woman.

Ana still didn't tell me about her reasons for quitting college.

But I would find out sooner or later.

She wanted to study since we were little kids, so for her to quit, it had to be something huge.

I knew Becky was in on the secret, but I didn't want to put her in a difficult position, so I didn't even ask about details.

She was as loyal to Ana as she was to Rachel and, lately, Vicky.

Those four were getting into trouble at every turn.

But neither I nor Mason really minded.

All four of them were happy and that's all that mattered at the end of the day.

There was also something going on with Vicky, but she wasn't willing to share either.

And the main concern for the past few months. Margareth. We had no idea where she was, but I was sure she was planning something awful and evil. But I guess we would just have to wait for her to approach any of us.

But right now, I had my focus on one woman alone.

My Becky.

Just when she popped into my mind she also popped into her house.

"Honey. I am home!"

She was my official assistant now and I had some difficulties preparing my surprise without her knowing.

But still, I managed.

So now I was standing in our living room, surrounded by red petals all over the floor, with a huge bouquet of roses in my hands and I was down on one knee.

She finally came around the corner and when she saw me, she dropped her purse and keys on the floor while her hands flew to her mouth.

"Becky, you know I am no good with romantic gestures, but I tried my best. And now I am asking you. Would you do me the Honor and become my wife?"

My question barely left my lips when she already managed to tackle me to the ground.

"Yes! Yes! Yes! I love you so much!"

I chuckled at her and managed to put a bit of space between us, so I could put a ring on her finger.

It looked good and made me feel proud.

When I looked at her, I could see she was deep in thought.

And I feared she was second-guessing her decision about marrying me.

But a second later she lifted her head and gave me her beautiful smile before she answered my unspoken question.

"I was just wondering when my life changed so much. I am the happiest woman alive right now, but just a few months ago I was JUST ANOTHER MODEL."

Oh, dear Becky. If only you knew how much more than just another model you truly are.

THE END

Stay tuned for 3rd story JUST ANOTHER NOTCH

ANA AND WILLIAM

Also, a short surprise awaits you at the beginning of the third book ☐

BOOK 3
JUST ANOTHER NOTCH


Ana

I was raised by my mother alone. My father passed away when I was still little.

All my life I just wanted to repay my brother and mother for all their support.

When I finally went to college, I never expected to find someone like him there.

As cliche as it sounds...it was love at first sight...at least for me.

But I learned the hard way, that the man I loved was a complete asshole.

Now I returned back home with my tail between my legs.

I managed to organize my life back to its previous perfection and almost got over William...

But I needed an investor for my business if I wanted to reach my goal.

And guess who turns out to be my silent partner? Yes. William the playboy himself.

Would I be able to resist him and his advances, or would I become just another NOTCH?


* * * * * * * * * * * * * *

William

I was ready to accept the arranged marriage my parents threw my way, when suddenly Ana appeared in my life.

She was perfect and I fell in love.

I wanted to tell her about my arranged marriage.

But how could I break the heart of the only woman I ever loved?

Suddenly my "bride-to-be" came to visit and ran into Ana, spewing bullshit about there being a date already on our wedding day, which was a total lie, but Ana didn't give me a chance to explain anything. She ran away from the college, from campus and most importantly, from me.

Now it happened she needed a silent investor, and I had a huge amount of money.

So why not make the one I love happy?

Sadly, she is convinced I just want to get her into my bed.

Could I convince her I love her, or would she turn her back on me and the future we could have.

Made in the USA
Columbia, SC
26 June 2024

37502789R00083